The Irish Dresser

A Story of Hope during The Great Hunger (An Gorta Mor, 1845–1850)

By
Cynthia G. Neale

WHITE MANE KIDS
SHIPPENSBURG, PENNSYLVANIA

This White Mane Books publication
was printed by
Beidel Printing House, Inc.
63 West Burd Street
Shippensburg, PA 17257-0708 USA

The acid-free paper used in this book meets the guidelines for
permanence and durability of the Committee on Production Guidelines for Book Longevity of the Council on Library Resources.

For a complete list of available publications
please write
White Mane Books
Division of White Mane Publishing Company, Inc.
P.O. Box 708
Shippensburg, PA 17257-0708 USA

Library of Congress Cataloging-in-Publication Data

Neale, Cynthia G., 1954-
    The Irish dresser : a story of hope during The Great Hunger (An Gorta
Mor, 1845-1850) / by Cynthia G. Neale.
        p. cm.
Summary: In the late 1840s as the potato famine spreads throughout
Ireland, thirteen-year-old Nora finds solace in the family's large
wooden cupboard where she dreams of cakes and other delicious things and
when her father decides that they should sail for America, the old
cupboard helps make her dreams come true.
    ISBN 1-57249-344-5 (alk. paper)
    1. Ireland--History--Famine, 1845-1852--Juvenile fiction. [1.
Ireland--History--Famine, 1845-1852--Fiction. 2.
Famines--Ireland--Fiction. 3. Emigration and immigration--Fiction. 4.
Ocean travel--Fiction.] I. Title.
    PZ7.N2546Ir 2003
    [Fic]--dc22
                                                    2003065787

Dedicated to the Shannonside Ceili Dancers of Rochester, New York, who first taught my heart and feet to make merry in Irish dance; to my mother, Doris; husband, Tim; and daughter, Hannah, who never wavered in their loving support; and to the Famine victims, who are not forgotten.

THE GREAT HUNGER
(*AN GORTA MOR*, 1845–1850)

Over one million Irish people perished from starvation and disease, and over two million had no choice but to leave Ireland and emigrate to new lands across the sea. Ireland, an English colony, was profoundly altered socially and culturally by the Famine. This event was one of the greatest human tragedies of the nineteenth century.

The Famine Irish were potato crop dependant, landless, and impoverished peasants, victims of British colonialism and racial hatred. Great Britain was one of the richest countries of the world and yet Ireland, thought to be rebellious and religiously lost for being Catholic, suffered this atrocity while one of their colonies. The disease that destroyed the potato crops was later identified as a fungus, receiving a Latin name: *Phytophthora infestans.*

This story is not written to declare the evil nature of one ethnic race over another, for all humanity at some time is guilty of prejudice. It is written for Famine descendants to remember the generational sorrow they have carried and not cried over, to honor the victims of the Famine, but mostly to rally hope and response to hunger crises around the world, especially in young readers' hearts.

Contents

Chapters

1 Miss Maggie Hen 1
2 The Cake 12
3 Potato Fog 24
4 Hunger 31
5 Boxty Cakes, Cornmeal, and a Magic Cow 46
6 Father 57
7 The Tumbling 61
8 Tickets to America 69
9 The Plan 77
10 Courage to Leave 81
11 Queenstown, Cork 85
12 Inside the Dresser 91
13 On Board the *Star* 100
14 Sailing Away from Home 104
15 A Stranger in the Dark 109
16 Adventure with a New Friend 116
17 Forgiveness 125
18 Hope 130
19 Almost America 135
20 The End and the Beginning 141
Epilogue 145
Glossary 147

Chapter One

MISS MAGGIE HEN

"A Cake! A Cake! There's going to be a Cake!" my sister and I sing together as we skip around our stone cottage on a hazy autumn afternoon. A patch of red poppies still blooms along the front, and as we pass by I notice their silky crepe petal skirts dancing in the wind. I spy amongst them bracken, those tall and spiky ferns, who become the perfect partners for the lady-like poppies.

A Cake, A Cake, we'll all partake!
A Cake, A Cake, for goodness sake!
A Cake, A Cake, and sweets galore!
A Cake, A Cake, 'til we can eat no more!

Ever since I can remember, there have been parties called "Cakes" in my village. There would be music, dancing, and sweets all afternoon and into the evening! It was as if we would climb out of our troubled dirty skin and dress ourselves with new glowing skin for a day. We became like selkies, those magical seals who left behind their human form to become sea creatures. Our feet that were always rooted to the earth with her labors would be plucked out for a day, scrubbed, and set to music.

My Da says the Cakes are for people who have fallen on hard times in Ireland. I wonder why we don't have a Cake once a week then, for it seems we

1

have all fallen on hard times. We live on small plots of land with only room for a garden of potatoes and some turnips, in cottages that were once our grandparents'. We live on our ancestors' land that is no longer our own. Da tells us stories about how the English took our land hundreds of years ago and have never given it back. Now we have to pay rent to them for the few acres we have. We dig our gardens with big old loys, which are large spades that make for backbreaking work. I remember last summer when the pestilence attacked the early potatoes before they were ever dug up. In the long wait for the October harvest, many people came down with the sickness. We have always lived mostly on potatoes, potatoes, potatoes. But not on Cake days!

"Miss Maggie Hen, there's to be a Cake at the O'Connors'!" I say to the fat, red, clucking hen roosting upon the thatched roof of our cottage.

The top half of the cottage door swings open and Meg, my sister who is fiery in hair and temper, yells out to me, "Miss Maggie Hen is nicely fattened for the slaughter, and just in the nick of time for the Cake."

"Away with you, Meg, you're a terrible sister to say so!" I answer.

Meg laughs and walks away from the opened half-door, leaving Kate and me wondering if she is speaking truthfully or in jest. My excitement over the Cake begins to disappear. I know most of our hens have gone to the landlord's table to help pay the rent. I miss the golden brown eggs we used to eat once a week. Sometimes Mam used the eggs to barter for buttons and salt on market day, but we'd always have some left over to eat. Now there is only Miss Maggie Hen, giver of many eggs, my beloved pet. Miss Maggie's eggs are no longer to be eaten at our table, however. We are now selling them in the market every week.

I am thirteen years old and the youngest in the McCabe family. I am much shorter than Kate, who is fourteen, and I barely reach beyond Meg's waist. Meg is the oldest, and has just turned sixteen. My dark brown hair is curly and wild, but Kate plaits it into one braid and adorns it with sprigs of honeysuckle. My eyes are a deep green, so green that my Da said they probably came from a mysterious mermaid of long ago. I've always thought of myself as being very dull looking, especially when I stand next to my two sisters. Kate is my favorite sister. She has been blessed with curly black hair, beautiful azure eyes, and an angelic face that doesn't have a freckle on it. Meg has radiant ginger hair and eyes filled with the blue of a clear summer sky. There are many days, like today, that Meg's eyes change into an angry summer storm. Her ivory freckles are scattered only over her nose and barely noticeable. My ugly freckles are the color of Meg's hair and plastered all over my face. They are as reckless on my face, my Mam claims, as I am throughout my days. I am all over the countryside getting into trouble, as are my freckles that scramble all over my face. I complained one day to my Mam that it seemed to me that I had been given Meg's freckles, for a ginger head such as hers should have freckles as bright as mine. Mam said that it had probably been a mix-up while we were being made in heaven.

"*Musha*, Nora," Mam said to me that day. "The angel in charge of such things was so blinded by the color of Meg's brilliant hair, she couldn't see and so she gave the freckles planned for you to Meg! And when you were getting ready to be born, the ones for our Meg were thought to go better with your lovely green eyes!" I really don't know if I believe Mam's explanation.

As Kate and I plead with Miss Maggie Hen to come down from the roof of our cottage, the hen only squawks and stays on her roost.

My Kate is a wisp of a girl and as delicate as a spring violet. I worry about her because she always has a cough, but Mam says there are many children in Ireland living with chest ailments because of the dampness. Kate is strong in other ways, such as in her love for others, and I never hear her complain of feeling ill.

I'm feeling sick in my belly because Meg said that Miss Maggie Hen has been fattened for the Cake. I yell at Meg, who is still in the cottage. I tell her that I am going to pull her ginger hair out of her cruel head! Kate comes to my side and tries to quiet my temper.

"No matter, Nora, never mind Meg and her ways," Kate says. "Miss Maggie Hen won't be at the Cake. We'll hide her in a crate with some straw down by the stream."

"Kate, you're brilliant!" I say to her as she runs to get a crate for Miss Maggie Hen.

I am always praying to the Blessed Mother to be as tender-hearted and gentle as Kate, but I never am. I certainly don't want to be like Meg, except maybe to be the oldest and as beautiful as she is. I think the birth angel had really gotten the orders mixed up. I should be a little bit of Meg and Kate, not altogether like I turned out. I don't think I'm like anyone in my family!

I pick one of the daisies that stick up between my toes.

"I am Meg," I say as I pull a petal from the daisy.

"I am Kate," I say as I pull out another petal. I pull out every petal, playing the game "he loves me not" with "I am Meg and I am Kate." When I finish pulling out all the petals, I look at the yellow center staring up at me.

"I am Nora!" I exclaim to the bright sunshine of the daisy that is its middle. I look into the foggy sky that seems to be blanketing my good feelings about the upcoming Cake, and say a prayer for it not to rain.

Meg opens both halves of the door of the cottage and walks out. The apron over her long flowered cotton dress is old and covered with stains from the wild strawberries she is pressing for jam.

"And don't I know that I have two lazy sisters who aren't helping me with putting up the jam? Mam's gone to the O'Connors' already and Da's gone to the big house. If we're to get ready in time for the Cake, come in for a sup of tea and finish this work I've already started."

"When did Mam and Da leave, Meg?" I ask.

"Early . . . even before the cock was up for his crowing. Now get Kate and hurry in so we can be on time," Meg says with authority.

"We'll be coming, Meg," I answer, looking to see where Kate is. My mind begins to wander to thoughts of the Cake as I stand waiting for my sister.

The O'Connors will have the tastiest and biggest decorated sugar cake this side of the sea. There will be whiskey and porter for the grownups; scones, tarts, and homemade bread for everyone. We'll be leaving our spuds in the pot at home for the 'morrow. We'll all have proper faces and manners for our neighbors. The musicians will play for the dancing into the wee hours of the night. Everyone will dress in their fancy clothes; all of us girls will decorate ourselves with a few ribbons and try to look as pretty as the cake itself! Everyone will bring something to raffle off, such as livestock and musical instruments. Oh, I don't know what we McCabes will be bringing. I hoped it wouldn't be Miss Maggie Hen! I did know that by the end of the Cake, the O'Connors' hard times would be over. They'd have enough money to cover paying for the party and for the cause of their troubles.

Kate comes back carrying an old wooden crate. I laugh to see her trying to lug a thing larger than herself.

"Kate, put it down! You'll bring harm to yourself. We can pull it with a piece of rope to the stream."

"Squawk, squawk!" cries Miss Maggie Hen, flying off the roof as if she knows she is to be held prisoner in the crate below her.

Kate sits down to rest upon the crate and motions for me to sit beside her.

"Why are the O'Connors in need of a Cake?" I ask.

"Meg says that poor Mr. O'Connor lost his cow off the cliff. It was his only means to pay the rent on Gale Day. Then his pig died . . . our pig's brother, Nora." Kate pokes me in my side, giggling, "That's why you shouldn't be naming the animals because they're never ours to keep. They must always be leaving us to pay the rent!"

"James the Pig is our own, Kate. He sleeps next to us almost every night. Will we have to give him up, too?"

"On Gale Day we will, and that's coming up soon."

"What's Gale Day?" I ask, screwing up my face so my freckles merge together.

Kate laughs at my face, "Oh, Nora, you've heard Da complain about it. It's a day when all over Ireland we who live on land that is already ours have to pay the landlord half the year's rent for it."

Suddenly the crate Kate and I are sitting on collapses and we fall into it. The wood splinters and Miss Maggie Hen begins fluttering around us squawking and carrying on, her feathers floating down to where we sit.

I pull myself out and reach for Kate. We laugh to see Miss Maggie Hen all flustered, but I am sure she is soon to become headless if we don't do something in a hurry.

"I've a grand idea, Kate. Why didn't I think of it before?" I exclaim.

"Tell me, Nora, quick, before Meg comes out again!"

"We'll put Miss Maggie Hen in the dresser! She'll quiet herself there because it's a cozy place where the fairies live."

"The fairies might not like Miss Maggie Hen in their cupboard and you don't want to anger them, as they'll be stealing away all our spuds." Kate's eyes tease with a glimmer in them.

"I'll have a chat with them then, before I put my Maggie in the dresser. They'll put her to sleep under their spell."

I half believe in fairies, as do most of the children I know. Da says the fairies are the *Tuatha De Danann,* a strange and mysterious folk, the original inhabitants of Ireland. When people called the Milesians came to Ireland, there was great confusion. It ended when the *Tuatha De Danann* agreed to live in fairy fortresses underground. I have always heard they were beautiful creatures, seeking good and pleasure, but easily angered if things don't go proper. I haven't really seen any fairies living in the dresser but I can imagine them there. Sometimes I feel their charms and believe that one day I'll set my eyes on one. There's hardly a day that passes without Mam scolding me for sitting in the dresser telling stories to them.

"Father O'Boyle wouldn't think it proper to be believing in ghosts and fairies when having the Holy Ghost should be enough," Mam said one day as I sat in the dresser.

Then Mam gave me some holy water and four-leaf clovers to put in the dresser to ward off any evil. I'm certain that if the good Lord can make the flowers of the field and Miss Maggie Hen, He certainly can make fairy folk.

Just then Miss Maggie Hen decides she is safe and won't be ending up in the crate. She stops flying around and tiptoes behind me, pecking at my old, flower-printed dress. I haven't told Mam about all the holes in my dress that Miss Maggie has already made, for she would be mad as a hen. Each of us has only two dresses, one for school and Mass and the other for every day.

"I'll go inside and ask Meg to come out to the garden with me. When we're in the garden, take Miss Maggie inside and hide her in the dresser," Kate whispers to me. Her lovely blue eyes are filled with mischievousness.

When Kate and Meg are looking at the potato plants teeming with dark green leaves and purple blossoms in the garden, I scoop the squawking Miss Maggie up and walk into the cottage. I shut the door and set Miss Maggie down upon the hard dirt floor that contains a few slabs of stone. She begins pecking and becomes irritated in striking only stone. I pull open the cupboard of the dresser and take out the crocks of drinking water and buttermilk. I am sorely tempted to take a drink of the delicious buttermilk, but I know Mam will notice if only a spoonful has been taken. I decide to take the crocks out to the stream in the shade and keep them there to stay cool. We do this every summer when it becomes too warm in the cottage to keep our perishables in the dresser. Mam will think it grand I did this without being told, for the days are still quite warm.

I sit down by the dresser and look at it with admiration. It has always been in our home, proudly standing next to the hearth. It's an Ulster dresser that seems to take up a whole wall of our cottage. It is made of pine and painted the color of blue morning glories. I love the elaborate designs in the fretwork at the top, and the sunbursts in the corners of the cupboards, and the simple beauty it has that seems to give our cottage a regal air. It was a wedding gift to Mam and Da from Mam's family in Dublin. This dresser has always been my special hiding place, though everyone knows when I am inside of it. It's not just a hiding place for my wee body, but a hiding place for my dreams. No one knows what I dream inside my magic dresser. Sometimes when I am there, I forget about all our troubles in Ireland. I love it most of all, even a bit more than Miss Maggie Hen.

Mam keeps her few pieces of Delph china in the dresser that we are never allowed to touch. Sometimes the china jiggles when I climb into the bottom of the cupboard of the dresser, but I always try to be careful. About a year ago, Da suggested we use the lower cupboard as a coop for our fowl. I was so angry at Da, I didn't greet him when he came in from his day's work. Mam was in tears, and after we girls were bedded down for the night, I heard Mam's harsh words that sounded like the gun fire of an overzealous hunter. Since that incident, there has never been another word about Da using the dresser to bed his animals in. I hope Mam won't find out about Miss Maggie Hen using it for a spell until after the Cake is over.

Inside the dresser, I am more with myself than when I am with myself anywhere else. I don't think even Kate understands this about me and the dresser. Sometimes I talk to God and the fairies when no one is in the cottage. I am always squeezing my eyes shut in a certain way, hoping to see a fairy, but if I do ever see one, I'm right sure I'll scramble out the door screaming for help. Even though I'm thirteen, I still fit in the dresser, being that I haven't been growing that fast. Or maybe the dresser magically expands when I climb into it.

Our cottage is small and built of large rough stones and mud. It has a front and back door with one small window that is covered with dried sheepskin at night. The roof is thatched with straw and rush with a hole for smoke from the hearth to escape. We sit on logs and flat stones around the hearth for our meals and storytelling, sometimes inviting our neighbors to join us. The butter churn sits next to the dresser, and the only other piece of real furniture is the creepie, which is the large stool where Da sits and plays his fiddle. This is his place in our home, but he is generous and always gives it up to a guest who comes for a sup of tea. Mam thinks it's grand we have a butter churn, as most farmers can't afford one. I don't think it's grand for all the work it takes me to make butter. My arms ache something fierce when it's my turn to spend the morning churning the cream into butter. Our cow, Miss Molly, has been sold now for months and I am no more complaining about all the churning, except when we get a bucket of milk from a neighbor once in awhile. The buttermilk I'm carrying was a gift from Mam's friend who owns two cows.

After I carry the buttermilk and water out to the stream and come back to the cottage, I notice Meg's strawberries and the jam she's been making that is sitting on a slab of stone next to the hearth. I quickly dip my finger into the wooden bowl to taste the berries and find they are so sweet and delicious! A friend who works at the big house has given Meg a small cone of sugar to use for the jam. She's a young Irish girl and a good friend to my ornery sister. I dip my finger in again and then see something out of the corner of my eye.

A mouse suddenly runs under the straw in the corner of the cottage where my sisters and I sleep together. Our only bedding is our shawls that we tie together at night to keep warm. I don't want a dirty field mouse crawling on them! Miss Maggie Hen begins flying around the cottage, and Mr. James Pig, who sometimes sleeps near us, jumps up, too. It's so dark in the cottage, I haven't even noticed Mr. James Pig was inside! I wonder how much of the preserves the mouse and Mr. James Pig have eaten!

"Out with you, Mr. James!" I yell as I open the bottom half of the front door to shove him out. Mr. James scoots out the door, barely able to fit, and I peer out at Kate and Meg standing in the garden. Meg's arms are crossed angrily in front of her. I have to hurry because Meg will never let Miss Maggie Hen stay inside the dresser. Heartless Meg will pick up Miss Maggie Hen, put her under her arm, and take her to the O'Connors' Cake!

I whisk Miss Maggie into the cupboard of the dresser and shut the doors. She lets out one long squawk and then becomes quiet.

"You must hush, Miss Maggie, and later I will bring you some seeds to eat. Tomorrow the Cake will be over and done with and I'll let you out."

I take a deep breath and kneel by the dresser and whisper, "My fair and lovely fairies . . . listen to my plea and keep Miss Maggie Hen safe in the dresser." I quickly make the sign of the cross and say, "Amen!"

I run out the door to the garden where Meg and Kate are still standing. Kate is holding some flowers and turnips in her hands, trying to convince Meg that the flowers are edible and will taste lovely with spuds. Meg is shaking her head madly and arguing with Kate, "the lot of us are likely to be killed eating such things!"

"It's a lovely day for a Cake, wouldn't you all agree?" I ask my sisters with a big smile on my strawberry-stained face.

"Oh God help ye, Nora McCabe, for you've been eating up all my hard work!" Meg screams at me as she tries to hit me with a branch she has quickly broken off the elderberry bush. I begin to run around the potato garden with Meg yelling after me and chasing me with the branch. I know I won't be caught, for I have just prayed to God's own fairies.

Chapter Two

THE CAKE

A young musician sits on a chair in the open air on a fine sunny day at the O'Connors'. He's a piper and playing one of my favorite tunes, "The Rakes of Mallow." A few of the old people are dancing around him. I stand next to him, awestruck as I watch his hands sweep the keys of his pipes with his great, long fingers. I know that James O'Brien is the son of a well-to-do farmer and is considered to be the best player in all of Munster. I have always thought of him as a very distinguished and handsome man, even though he is a few years beyond my own.

I look around and don't see Da anywhere. I'm anxious for him as he works too hard and has little rest. I'm afraid he'll miss the Cake and being able to play his fiddle with the musicians. By now, he should have been accompanying James O'Brien on the pipes. I begin to walk around the O'Connors' house and greet all our neighbors who have come to partake in the Cake. I see Mam busy with the other women placing food on a crooked, old wooden table in front of the cottage. I've heard it said of women in Ireland that they have an eternal station at the hearth. I shudder to think that someday it will be my turn to be at the hearth all day, too. I think I already spend too much time there helping Mam and my sisters prepare our food. As I watch the food being placed on the old table, I wonder if Mam will see me and ask me to help. I don't want to have to work on this special day and so I hide behind the corner of the cottage to watch everything. I'm pleased to see Mam out of doors with the wind blowing through her wisps of hair that have fallen around her face. Her face is creased from all the hard living she has done, the lines telling stories of her life. I am saddened by what I see on her face, as if the harshness of her life has left an imprint that can't be erased. And then I wonder if Mam would be happy if she were unable to work as she does. Even my Meg is like Mam, as they both delight in being queen of the hearth, but not me. I do not like being confined to the cottage and would rather run through the fields. As I watch Mam, I think she is more beautiful than any of the other mothers in my village.

"Come, Nora, let's go see the cake!" yells Kate, who comes running alongside me with two of the O'Connor children, Eileen and Padraic, who are nine and ten.

I decide to take the chance of Mam seeing me so I can get a look at the cake. As we walk through the crowd, we are jostled and greeted by everyone, "*Dia Dhuit, Dia Dhuit* [Hello, God Be With You!]" everyone shouts to us with merriment.

I notice that there are people from the surrounding villages that have come to the Cake, too, for they look familiar even though I can't remember their names. They live like us and grow potatoes to eat every day of their lives. I suppose it's a blessing that the golden potato, the lumper, is more easily grown than any other food. Mam calls it a staple for all of us. I twirl in the air as I walk across the grass, for I feel my mouth water for all I'd be eating this day! I know about all the scrumptious food the landlords and the people in the big houses eat in Ireland. My sisters and I make up songs about all that food—mutton, beef, cakes, sauces, and jam tarts! But now I was at a Cake and I'd be eating more than just potatoes and buttermilk, lumper potatoes and buttermilk! And Mam has promised we'll have some of Miss Maggie's eggs for breakfast tomorrow! Yesterday, she had taken some of Miss Maggie's eggs to the market to trade for a salt-box and a knife-box for our cottage and there had been eggs left over. Oh, it was a grand day with the woodbine creeping along the cottage wall, the birds chirping to the piper's notes, and the Cake just beginning! I begin skipping with the children towards the table where the cake sat.

When we come to the table, I gaze at all the breads, especially the barm brack. Barm brack is my favorite bread of all! It's made with sugar, spices, and dried fruit, and is usually served for weddings. I wonder if there's a ring, a rag, a bean, or a pea in it. If there is a ring, maybe our Meg will get it and be married in a year! I hope I get the pea and then I'll never have to marry and work eternally at the hearth. The pea foretells wealth. I'll be really well off! We don't have to worry about anyone getting the bean. It means that the person who gets the slice with the bean in it will come to poverty, and Mam said we already have that one.

"Away to your Mam to give her a hand!" one of the mothers yells at us as we try to taste some of the food. I see Mam looking at me as she carries out the colcannon. I'll be sure to stay away from any of that! It is made with potatoes, butter, milk, and cabbage. Then I see some stew that has been made with real mutton! Where did all this food come from? None of us have done really well for ourselves to have food like this that is fit for kings. I can't wait to eat, but I run from the table so Mam won't call me to work next to her.

Kate and I hurry to join all the children crowding around the most special treat of all, the ornamental cake, which stands alone upon an upturned butter churn. On the odd-looking churn is spread a white, homemade linen towel of Mrs. O'Connor's in which the cake sits upon, looking like a bride. The cake is covered with sugar icing and has tiny sweet violets decorating the top and cascading down the sides. I know it's a special cake from the baker in town who makes the tallest cakes in my parish. It is almost three feet high! Kate and I squeeze in amongst the children to get nearer to the cake, but suddenly my arm is grasped. I turn to see who is tugging and hurting my arm. It's my own mean sister, Meg.

"There you are, Nora! I told Kate to tell you to come along after me and bring the hen. You were dilly-dallying and I couldn't wait any longer. Where is that hen of yours, Nora?" Meg asks. I notice that Meg's beautiful hair is hidden under an old, discolored head scarf. The scarf is navy blue with tiny pink flowers that look old and dirty. I can't believe my Meg wears such a thing when her hair is as beautiful as a crown of spun gold.

"Miss Maggie Hen was nowhere to be found," I lie, dropping my head.

Meg takes me by the shoulders and stares hard into my eyes, her jaw set. "You're full of brilla-bralla, Nora McCabe! Mam and Da depend upon me to take care of these things. How disgraced we'll be without something for the raffle. Da will be getting another hen next week, but it's today we are needing something for the Cake!" She shakes me hard and turns away with tears in her eyes.

I can feel my face redden with my lie, but I must convince Meg to not give Miss Maggie away. I walk in front of Meg and plead with her to listen.

"Meg, don't worry, I have something for the raffle. I've already thought of what I can do in exchange for Miss Maggie Hen!"

I reach into my pocket and pull out my special comb with the intricate interlocking circles and curves decorating it. It always makes me feel that my dull brown hair is pretty when I wear it.

"This is for the raffle, Meg!" I exclaim.

"It's your only piece of finery," Meg says, "and you'll not be borrowing mine! I've a notion to send you home to fetch Miss Maggie Hen, for I know you're hiding her from me!"

"Please, Meg, be kind to Nora and use her things for the raffle. Miss Maggie Hen will give us more eggs, and Da can save his money on another hen," Kate pleads.

"If Da knows we didn't give the hen for the O'Connors' raffle, he might be shamed. The O'Connors might think he's close-fisted and using his own daughter's belongings to pinch a penny."

"With all the hens clucking at this Cake, how will anyone know which one came from where!" Kate answers.

"All right, then, but Nora will have to tell the truth when we'll be 'round the hearth for the evening prayers," Meg says.

"I promise I'll tell Da the truth, and God, too," I say with a relieved smile on my face. I am suddenly filled with hope for Miss Maggie and for the delicious food we'd soon be eating. I grab Meg's and Kate's arms and try to get them to dance a three-hand reel with me.

Meg was reluctant, her body unyielding to my touch and the dance. I look at her and marvel how she could be so hard. Her lips are always fixed in determined resolution, and they rarely smile. I can't remember when I last saw my Meg dance.

"Come on, then, Meg . . . 'tis time to pick up your skirts and make your feet happy!" I cry out.

Meg finally relinquishes her grave sobriety and leaps into the dance with full abandon, holding hands with Kate and myself. The people at the Cake encircle us and begin to clap to the music and our sprightly dancing. When the musicians finish the tune, everyone applauds and I know we look radiant. "What a day to remember," I think with satisfaction.

Just then, there is a stirring in the crowd, the musicians stop playing, and everyone begins to whisper. My sisters and I look all around for Da and Mam but can't find them. The joy I have just felt suddenly leaves me and there is a threatening dark cloud hanging over the Cake and all of us.

People are looking and pointing to where Father O'Boyle is standing with Parson Milford at his side. They both look glum and I know they must be bringing bad news to the O'Connors' Cake. The villagers don't look too pleased to see the two men together. Most everyone in the surrounding villages is Catholic and everyone in Ireland is under the domination of the English, who are Protestant. The Protestants and Catholics seldom befriend one another. Our Father O'Boyle of St. Joseph's Catholic Church is a different sort of man, a unique person, my Mam says. Parson Milford, as Protestant as can be, is a minister for the Church of Ireland. He and Father O'Boyle are great friends, and just about everyone in the village has come to accept this, but not all. There are some men in our villages involved in the secret societies and are determined to bear arms against the English landlords. Da says they're savages and destroy the property of the landlords, and have even murdered some of the landlords who were riding in their carriages down the road! We all despise the tithe that we have to pay to the Church of Ireland every year, but my Da says there are peaceful ways to fight the English.

I've heard my Da complain bitterly about it, "And don't I know that we need to be keeping our own priest in his parish with the little money we offer him. It is a pity to pay tithe to the Protestant church when we're ruled by the likes of those attending there! We have nothing to do with their religion!"

I feel frightened to see the priest and parson look so angry and serious. As I look away from their disturbed faces, I see my Da standing to the far right of them. His fiddle is leaning upon his leg and the bow is in his hand. He looks like he has spied a ghost at the Cake. I catch his eye and he looks hard at me. I wonder for a moment if he has found out about the lying I've done over Miss Maggie Hen! My heart is beating so fast, I feel everyone can hear it.

"We are saddened to have to make a grave announcement at the O'Connors' Cake, but it is needful for all here to know the criminal matter before us," Father O'Boyle speaks loudly to the crowd.

"There has been regrettable vandalism done to the parson's home and church. All of his livestock have been stolen, his furniture has been broken up into small pieces, and most sadly, the church is covered in blood from some of his animals they slaughtered. Axes have hewn the pews into useless lumber, and the congregation now has nowhere to worship."

"Let them come to your church, then, Father!" shouts someone from the crowd. Laughter erupts amongst a few of the men sitting near me.

"Let them sit under the hawthorn tree, amongst the nettles, then, for their worshipping!" cries out another.

Though I am relieved the interruption at the Cake has nothing to do with me, I am saddened to hear of this terrible destruction. There is hatred and frustration against the English ruling over us, but this will only make things worse. We will all be unjustly blamed, and it will mean a higher rent added to our already high one. The crowd begins murmuring. Sympathy is hard to find amongst us for any kind of hardship the Protestants suffer!

"Can you find it in your heart, lads, to lay down your prejudice and help this man and his family? He, like me, is trying to serve God and the flock given to him to shepherd. The people of his congregation are locked up in their homes, for written in blood upon the walls are some of their names and accusations against them. Do you realize that this atrocity will bring injustice to all of us? Might I plead with you this day to lay down your hate, forget that some of them have more to eat and wear than you do, and bring yourselves to help?"

Someone in the crowd yells, "To hell with the dirty Prods!"

The villagers begin whispering amongst themselves. Father O'Boyle and Parson Milford stand silently staring out at the crowd. I think to myself that they look like two village stone statues depicting some long-forgotten story in history. I look over at Da as he picks up his fiddle and walks towards the musicians. Meg and Kate take hold of my hands and we stand waiting for some sign from him as to what to do now that the grand, longed-for Cake is to be no longer frivolous and, especially, tasty.

Da speaks with the musicians and then walks over to Father O'Boyle and Parson Milford. After talking to these men of God for a few moments, we then see him raise his hand to silence the villagers who have become loud and agitated.

"With the blessing of the O'Connors, I say we all go to Parson Milford's and have the Cake there!" Da says with enthusiasm and sureness. I feel my cheeks flush in pride over my father's kind words. Meg and Kate squeeze my hands. They, too, are proud of him, as we all know how much he hates paying tithe to the parson's church.

The villagers cheer, and I wonder about the men who had yelled out cruelty against the Protestants. Did they change their minds? I am puzzled until I remember something special about my people. We can be beaten down by the weariness of poverty and hardship, but we are compassionate, and ready to halve our only potato with anyone who comes along our way, even a dirty Prod. I'm sometimes terribly confused about this good part of us that can still live with hate that seeks revenge and murder in trying to obtain freedom. Mam is always telling us that truth and light will reign over evil and darkness, and some-day the beauty and truth of Ireland will be known.

Most of the villagers at the Cake hurry home to change from their fancy clothes to everyday work clothes in order to work at Parson Milford's. Later, enough proceeds are raised from the raffle to pay for the O'Connors' loss, and the Protestant church is cleaned and repaired by the loving hands of the Catho-lic villagers. The day seems to never end as I scrub and help feed the people. I'm beginning to think I've already arrived at this eternal place of the hearth.

By the time I've come to think I'll be a slave forever, the glorious cake is presented by the light of a full moon. The icing has hardened as the evening cooled, and there are a few violets that have blown away in the wind. Every bite is as sweet and memo-rable as the Day of the O'Connors' Cake held at Par-son Milford's Protestant church.

"Da, I have a confession to make," I say later in the evening when the dancing has begun, interrupting him as he plays with the musicians.

"'Tis the priest then you must be seeing tomor-row, me pet," he says with laughter in his eyes.

"I'm dead serious, Da!" I say with sadness. "I lied to Meg and hid Miss Maggie Hen away in the dresser so she wouldn't be given to the O'Connors. She's my own, Miss Maggie Hen is, and I beg you to let me keep her!" My tears spill down my face from all the pent-up feelings of the day.

Da's face grows solemn and he's silent for a time, the musicians playing on without him.

"Is this why I heard the scratching in the dresser cupboard this noon, Nora? It was Miss Maggie Hen? I was ready to tell you that the fairies had come to dwell there after all!" he says. I stop crying and look at Da, but I can't tell whether he's angry or not, his eyes warmly looking into my own.

"I took the hen out of the dresser, Nora," Da says, and I tremble as I look into his face, wondering if Miss Maggie had been given to the O'Connors after all.

"Your sister, Meg, pleaded with me to leave the hen at the cottage. She cried the tears of a baby for your sake when she saw I had found the hen. Then she told me what you had given away to save the life of that ignorant hen. Your lovely hair piece to adorn your hair with, Nora! It was then, pet, I thought to myself that if my Nora can love a stupid animal with such passion that she can give away something of value, how great her life will be when she's grown, for she'll know how to sacrifice for love."

I can't fully understand how my wrong could become so right in my Da's eyes, but I know it's true that I love Miss Maggie Hen and my family with all my heart. I jump into my Da's lap and hug his neck.

Da hugs me back, and then he says, "'Tis wrong to lie for a good reason, Nora, and I'll not have you turning it into a habit. You're to come to me, Nora, and tell me your thoughts. And you must not get yourself so attached to the beasts that come our way. We can never keep them! You'll be smothering those animals with so much love, they'll be talking back to the grand ones at the big house. And then where will we be, for the likes of them will be taking it out on us by raising our rent!" I know that Da is teasing with me, but I'm still to take him serious.

I leave my Da and the musicians to where the children are playing hopscotch with a skipping rope. Whoever can keep skipping the longest without stopping wins a prize—a tart given by one of our mothers caring for the food.

After a time, I see Meg walking by and I run to thank her for crying real tears for me, as I now know that my own mean sister must love me after all! Then I notice she isn't wearing the old head scarf and her hair is flowing down her back and shining in the moonlight. I see something shimmering in her long ginger hair. It's my hair comb with the beautiful designs!

I run to her and try to pull the comb from her hair.

"Nora, are you mad? Away from me, you foolish girl!" cries Meg, pushing my hand away.

"You never raffled my hair piece but kept it for your own! I'm telling Da, Meg! How could you do this to me!" I yell at her.

"Hush, Nora, you're too much of a baby with your feelings falling out of you all the time," Meg says.

I try to quiet myself, but it is difficult, as usual. My feelings are forever coming out of me without my control.

"I did give the O'Connors your hair piece for the raffle." Then I notice how Meg lifts her head high and her voice changes when she tells me what happened. "Later, the piper, Mr. James O'Brien, came to me and asked if I would remove the old scarf from my hair. At first, I told him no, but then I took the scarf off and he presented me with your comb for my hair! He had won it in the raffle and gave it to me as a token of his affection. I couldn't tell him it was my own sister's comb." Meg's face isn't wearing her usual severity and she's actually smiling sweetly at me.

"Don't worry, Nora, I'll take good care of it," Meg says dreamily as she walks away.

Later that evening after returning to our cottage, and everyone is sleeping, I creep to the dresser to listen for the fairies. When I think I hear something, I open the door and try to see inside. There is light coming from the moon through the window. As I peer into the cupboard of the dresser, I see my beautiful comb, still sparkling from the moon beams having touched it! I carefully take it out of the dresser and put it in my hair. Then I climb onto the straw bed next to my sisters and give Meg a gentle kiss upon her cheek. I lie down and fall asleep, dreaming of the loveliest Cake I've ever attended in my life.

Chapter Three

POTATO FOG

"I believe in God, the Holy Ghost, and some of his fairies . . . ," I utter, half-asleep on the bed of straw next to my sisters. Meg is awake and nudges me to keep quiet. Kate is sleeping soundlessly. Meg is used to hearing me talk in my sleep, and as she is telling me to keep quiet, I see her smile when she notices the comb in my hair that she hid in the dresser for me. The early morning hour for all of us to rise has not yet come, but I'm suddenly stirred by an unusual scent in the air. I yawn and a foul odor gets stuck in my throat. I think it must be from the rain in the bog emitting a stench. I look nervously at Meg and shake Kate to awaken her. Kate moans and turns over, a dry cough beginning to take hold of her. Meg begins to fall back to sleep. I am alone with thoughts of the evil spirit, the *taise*. I have been told not to worry for such a thing, but I have sat around the hearth with storytellers who have told of this apparition that comes to warn of an accident, or to show an image of oneself, which means that you will soon die. "Oh, God, help me, help me, help me," I whisper, with terrible pounding fear in my whole body. It's only when the night has rubbed itself against the moon's face, and there is absolute still-ness, that I finally fall into a deep sleep.

A few hours later, Meg, Kate, and I awake to an eerie silence. We sit up and can see in the dim light

24

of the cottage that there is no fire in the hearth, Mr. James Pig is still sleeping near us, and Mam and Da are gone! Panic seizes us, as this is not the familiar order of our Sundays, unless, of course . . .

"Listen!" I cry out. We stand up, shivering in our tattered petticoats, listening for the sound of the fog we fear has come to try and starve us again. It had come to Ireland before and tried to suffocate and deaden our lives.

Mr. James Pig stirs, struggles to stand, and snorts loudly. I walk to the door to let him out, but stop when Kate cries out, "The birds aren't singing and there's a foul smell to the air!"

Quickly we dress, light our candles, and walk outside with Mr. James Pig following close behind. The stench in the air is strong and it takes our breaths away. The air is cool and moist, as it has been raining throughout the night. The sun seems unwilling to shine, for the clouds have smothered its rays and stand guard over what is to be a great devastation in our land. I know then that I have been right! An evil spirit had come in the night to warn me of danger! My sisters and I walk to our garden of potatoes, and I scoop up Miss Maggie Hen for comfort on our way. As we get closer to the garden and the source of the putrid odor, we see our Mam kneeling in the dirt that is sodden with the night's rainfall.

"The potato fog has come, girls. We'll be needing to save what we can for the harvest. Your Da has gone to tell the neighbors. Get on your knees with me, quick! Cut away the dead stalks, take out the stones, save the green ones!" Mam is drenched and covered with dirt and the rot from the potatoes. Kate and Meg begin tearing away in the garden, falling to their knees like Mam. I feel ill in my belly, ready to heave any moment. I set Miss Maggie Hen down, and she squawks and runs away.

"I'm to be ill, Mam. I can't . . . ," I cry.

"You'll not be pitying yourself now, child!" Mam says, and pulls my arm to force me to come. I resist, and fall onto some rotting potatoes and then become ill all over myself. I can't stop crying as I try to find the good plants amongst the discolored and dead ones.

"Go on with ye, Nora, go to the spring and bring us some water so we can wash off this stench. Make yourself useful, for you are of no use in this garden!"

I am dizzy, wet, and foul-smelling, but what is worse is that I'm ashamed of being so weak and afraid. My family is in the mud and rain trying to save our potatoes, and I can't help. The potato blight had come the year before and half destroyed our potato crop and the crops of our neighbors. Some said it was punishment because we Irish are gluttonous and eat too many potatoes. I know better even though I'm just a child. We have nothing else to eat except potatoes! And I think about the wheat, oats, and barley that are grown here in Ireland. My mind races with thoughts of our plight. I know my Da labors to grow these grains, but he says they're grown not for us, but for the English, for workers in the grand factories and for their families. Sometimes Da brings home the grain left over from the fields he has worked in, and Mam makes yummy breads.

There'll be no grain for us to eat now that our spuds are rotten to the core! Panic seizes my belly and chest. I think of the lovely Cake we have just partaken of and long to live the day again. I think of harvest time when a pig is slaughtered and the landlord has been paid his rent, and we have fancy food to eat. Most of our meals are potatoes and buttermilk, potatoes and buttermilk, but we have always given thanks.

I stumble across the field unable to stop my mind from rushing to and fro with all sorts of thoughts about Ireland and our family. We Irish know that the potato is our blessing and so we make meals out of it that are fit for kings in our small cottages. I know the potato is the strength of my people. And I also know the potato is the curse of my people when it fails to thrive. With heaviness in my heart, I think about the grain that is grown by my Da's hands in the landlord's fields and how it will still flourish while our potatoes rot, and none of it will be given to us to ease our hunger!

I walk and then crawl to the spring, pulling a bucket behind me. My petticoat is filthy, my tears won't stop streaming down my face, and I am filled with fear and anger. The spring is only down the hill behind our cottage but it seems to take me forever to get there. When I finally reach the spring, I fill the bucket with water, and then hear a sound behind me. As I turn to look, I am surprised to see the landlord's agent on his horse! It's Mr. Beale! Everyone hates this man, as he is evil with only one passion. The passion for the silver he receives from the landlord who is never in Ireland, but stays far away in England. He takes care of the landlord's land, and that includes us on that land, as if we were his cattle! Da says Mr. Beale couldn't find work before he came here because he had been in debtor's prison in England. He is a rogue, but he hates us and calls us lazy papists working in our lazy beds of spuds.

"You, over there!" he yells at me, "Come here so I can have a good look at you!"

I drop the bucket of water I have just filled and feel my legs give out underneath me. As I fall in a heap on the ground, I hear his horse snort loudly and I am frightened that this wicked man is going to ride right over my trembling body. Instead, I hear laughter as he rides away, uttering, "Filthy papist swine!"

Early in the evening just before the day gives out, the O'Connors come to our cottage to sit around the hearth. All the day the birds have stayed hidden and the dogs have howled at the displeasing odor of the rotting potatoes.

"Only yesterday it was, John, we had lush gardens. All of us! The plants are diseased. 'Tis come again!" Da says to his friend and neighbor, John O'Connor.

"These potatoes will always be giving us torment, Eoin. And don't we all know there should be another way of surviving than growing spuds," John says.

"Any of the neighbors salvage their crops, do you know, John?" Da asks.

"But a few, but a few . . . just a handful like us. I was forever tearing up the gangrene stalks and their blackened and withered leaves, but as soon as I did, the ones next to them turned black before my eyes!" John covered his face with his hands.

I am in the dresser listening to their conversation. Wearied and feeling I might perish like our spuds, I managed to carry the bucket of water to Mam. I never told Mam about the agent, Mr. Beale. She'll tell Da and he'll get so angry, he might threaten the agent's life. Da is really a peaceful man and despises the Irishmen who join the secret societies to fight the English, but I also know Da respects his own strength and temper. It is there. I've seen it come out of him in a fury. He says he needs to rein it in and save it for when it's needed the most. I'm certain Da's threats will make the agent kill Da instead, as he is the one with the gun. I can't say anything about the episode at the stream. It's the second time this past week that the agent has come upon me when I've been away from our cottage.

I feel safe in the dresser, in spite of what this dark day has brought. My belly is still in knots and my legs feel like jelly, but Mam gave me a kiss on the cheek and I know I'm forgiven for carrying on as I did when we found our diseased spuds this morning. Only a few of the spuds have been saved and we put them in the storage area above our sleeping corner that still holds a few from last year's harvest. Mam and Mrs. O'Connor are now cooking a few on the hearth. The O'Connors and all of us McCabes have gathered strength by working side by side during this terrible day, and we don't want to take our leave from one another in the darkness of a sorrowful evening. I know Mam and Da are trying to be strong in front of us children as they go about preparing an evening around the hearth with the neighbors. They're trying to act as if the potato fog has never come.

When the spuds have been cooked, the pot is taken off the fire, drained, and set upon the stool. There are a few screws of salt and mustard that are placed in the middle of the floor. We begin dipping our potatoes in the salt and mustard and eat yet another meal of potatoes.

"There is nothing like praties and a dab at the stool," Da says aloud, trying to sound cheerful. Everyone smiles weakly and tries to be jovial, but it is difficult. I have come out of the dresser to eat, but each bite is like a lump in my belly. "Maybe that's why they're called lumper potatoes," I think grimly, "as they're eaten with lumps in our throats and fall like lumps in our bellies."

"I sold my fishing lines last year when the pestilence came and nearly destroyed all of our crops. If only I had them now, we'd be going fishing to help us through this," Da says.

"Tomorrow, all of us children can go looking for some pignuts and mushrooms, Da," Meg says with confidence. Perhaps the attention Meg received from Mr. James O'Brien is giving her hope, as I still see something different about her since the Cake. The Cake! It was only yesterday that the sun must have used up all its light and glory to shine on the Cake, and now there is none left over for the rest of our days. I feel a sob come into my throat, but push it down with another lump of potatoes. I tell myself I must not become a baby again.

Mam raises herself stiffly off a log by the hearth. She walks to the dresser and takes out a tin of holy water. She begins praying and flicking it into all of our faces while we sit around the hearth. We all make the sign of the cross and pray silently. Mam and Mrs. O'Connor begin weeping, and it gets louder as if they're keening at a wake.

Da stands up and opens the half door to look out into the damp darkness of night. I look over at him and he turns to all of us and says, "From the English we'll have a multitude of problems, legislation that won't help us, and little food, if any. Ireland is my dark Rosaleen and her poetry and music are fading away from her. It's over there in America we'll need to be going instead of giving the pig for the rent to the landlord!"

I crawl back into the dresser and everyone but John O'Connor and Da are weeping bitterly. I think that our weeping is not only because of the loss of our potatoes, and the hunger we know we'll be having, but also for the loss of our land. I try to fall asleep in the dresser by waiting for the fairies to come. I reach up to touch my hair and it is then that I realize my comb has been lost. With the frenzied rain coming down from the potato fog, it will never be found.

"Maybe in America, thanks be to God and his fairies, I'll have a lovelier comb for my hair," I say as hope rises in my heart and lulls me to sleep.

Chapter Four

HUNGER

Ever since the potato fog came to Ireland, I am always frightened and hungry. I am as hungry as a caterpillar devouring the leaves on a branch of a tree. My hands shake while I pick berries from the wet fields and eat them. It had been October when the potato fog came and destroyed our crops. Now it is November and it has been raining every day since, a soft drizzle that makes us all feel like creatures of the sea. Our skin is always moist, just like seals, just like fish.

All over Ireland, the potatoes have turned into a blackened mass of corruption, becoming rotting and putrid mush as we pick them. My family only rescued a few from our garden. They were small ones, as they had not completely ripened. These have already been eaten. We had some potatoes in storage from the year before but they have been given away to our neighbors who had none left in their storage. It has always been difficult in the summer months before the fall harvesting of the potatoes, even before this blight. Many of the men travel to other parts of Ireland to find extra work during the summer months. The women are left to scour the countryside for berries, nettles, and other vegetables to put in the pot with a fist of grain, if they have any. This year it is worse, for there will be no harvesting of any potatoes! And I can't understand why no one talks about going to America as they did on the night the potato fog came. I don't think I really want to go there, but I want to hear grownups talk about hope, for it seems to be as sparse as the potatoes are in Ireland.

It has been almost three weeks since my family and I ate our last potatoes. We still comb through our garden looking for healthy ones, but I never find any that aren't rotten. Meg thought Kate meant what she said about eating turnips with some flowers, and tried cooking them together. The taste was bitter, but it only made us feel slightly ill. Now we are all waiting for our Da to return from the Relief Works. When Da left for the Works a few days ago, I lost all control of myself and clung to his pant leg.

"Da! Don't go! You'll never come back to us. Wouldn't it be grand if we could go to America!" I cried bitterly. It was a well-known fact that some fathers never returned from the Works.

My Da, Eoin McCabe, is a tall, handsome, and dark-haired man. He is thin from his meager diet, and his face is creased with many lines from working outside all his days. I think he is desperately trying to stay in the dearest place to him and his family—Ireland—and going to the Relief Works is his last attempt to make some money to buy grain and some seed potatoes to harvest for the following year. I have heard Da tell Mam that the rent has been paid until October, but that he doesn't know how it will be paid after that. I know Da's mind has been seized with worrying about all of his family. The schools in Ireland are closing, as children have been too weak to learn anything with the pangs of hunger attacking them all the time. All we did now was hunt like the beasts of the field looking for food. Our learning has been stopped and our hunger has increased.

"I'll be coming home, pet," Da had answered when I pleaded with him not to go to the Works. "Mr. O'Connor and I will be off to the Relief Works to build more useless roads. The English have decided to help us in our loss by giving us work on the roads, and so we'll be making money to rent our own land. All the while, there is food here still grown for English bellies, but not for our own, after the spuds have rotted before their merciless eyes."

"Then I'll go and help, too, Da," I cried, "for there's no more school and Meg and Kate can stay to help Mam."

Da lifted me onto his lap, "No, Nora, 'tis no place for a wee child like yourself. It is hard work for strong men only." I stared into my Da's face and could see that he was no longer a strong man. He is so thin, just like a stick figure, a clown on stilts wearing an oversized ragged coat with tails. Mam had found Da a French swallow-tailed dress coat a few years ago in the market. She had bartered a hen to buy it for Da as a surprise. He has never felt comfortable in it and only wears it on special occasions. When I saw him wear it the day he left for the Relief Works, I knew his leaving was important for all of us.

On the day Da left for the Relief Works, the rain continued to pelt our cottage as my heart broke. The gnawing in my belly ached something fierce, but the loss of Mr. James Pig and Miss Maggie Hen had been almost worse than my hunger. My Da was gone and I was close to fainting away altogether because of the pain in my heart and belly. I had climbed into the dresser clutching one of Miss Maggie Hen's feathers and Da's fiddle. He didn't know where his fiddle had gone, for I had hidden it in the dresser when he started talking about selling it. Miss Maggie Hen and Mr. James

Pig had been sold to pay the rent for Gale Day. Just as I thought, the rent had increased because the criminals who had vandalized Parson Milford's church and home had never been found. We were all blamed for the evil deeds of some of our people. Mr. James Pig had not brought in enough money for the rent, but Mr. James Pig and Miss Maggie Hen together were just enough. Da told me to think of Miss Maggie Hen as the best friend I ever had, for she gave herself up for us to have a home.

As I pick a few small berries, I think about Da, Miss Maggie, and Mr. James all having left me. I am in such deep thought, I don't realize that I have stuffed some of the stems of the blackberries into my mouth. I cry out in pain, for there are small prickly thorns that cut my mouth. As I spit everything out, I am startled that my blood is mixed in with the red stain of the berries. I feel sick in seeing my own blood, and quickly wipe my berry-stained hands on my apron, and hurry to go home across the field. Mam and my sisters are still out looking for things to eat, scouring the fields surrounding our cottage. I feel cold and aware of the hunger that never goes away. It is like an evil spirit that is always tormenting me.

As I walk, I suddenly hear a quiet, but strong voice tell me to go to the landlord's big house to take a peek inside. I think I must be going mad! Are the fairies speaking to me? Have I prayed to hear them for so long that now I have a wicked one speaking to me? I wonder who will be at the big house. I know the agent, the help, or someone will be there living life normally, even if the landlord is away in England. I'm longing to see what they have to eat on their table. My mind swirls with thoughts about peering in to get a good look at the food. I need to know that there is such grand food to be had someday for myself and all of us. I need to know there is food in Ireland besides these nettles and berries that never fill the emptiness in my belly. I have begun to think the whole world is starving. I need to know that somewhere in this land there is bread and meat!

I change my direction across the field and head down the hill where I know the big house sits like a magic castle. There is a power in my body and mind that I have not known before. I need to do this one thing and then I will be able to go home to my own hearth and eat whatever Mam has prepared for our evening meal.

I also think of the times I've walked by the big house with my sisters, but I have never really gotten close to it. It looked like a stone prison to my young eyes, and I was glad to not live in such a place. As I meander over another hill and get closer to the grand house, I notice the ivy growing around its turrets and the flower beds ablaze with color. There's a stone fence all around the grounds that is more than half my height. I see the gate, and on either side of it are ugly stone faces with gaping mouths, half lion and half man, staring at me. They're standing guard, and I'll not be able to get in or climb over such a high fence! I decide to walk to the back of the house to try and see into the kitchen where there'll be servants preparing food.

Maybe Molly, Meg's friend, will be there and invite me in for a sup of tea, I think. My stomach cramps up when I think of the food I'd be seeing, and I suddenly have to spit up saliva that has rolled up into my throat and mouth. I don't see anyone, but there is a carriage sitting in the front and the horses are stomping their feet. I try to be quiet as I crouch along the stone fence to get to the back where the kitchen will be. Mam always said the only difference between the people living in the grand big houses and ourselves is the houses themselves, and, of course, all the food they eat. "Fat old women layered in lace and petticoats live in those castles and they can't move in their fancy clothes to run through a field," I utter quietly to myself. My Kate and I have laughed over the sight of them.

My heart is almost pounding out of my chest. Will the agent appear and flog me? He has flogged some children in my village and almost made a cripple out of poor William O'Dyer. I try to hurry because I must look into the kitchen to see all the preparations going on for the grand dining room! Even with all my fear, I must see the food! As I near the corner to the back of the house, I hear voices, terrible voices, voices that seem to be crying. I get down on my knees and begin crawling closer to the fence and around the corner of the house.

"*Ocras! Ocras!*" wail five people standing at the fence facing the kitchen. I am shocked to see that their bodies are ghost-like, withered, and small.

Are they children? I wonder.

I soon realize that these are grownups who have become like desperate children in their hunger. I don't think they're anyone from our village. They have come from other places where the potato blight has already been before it came to us.

"*Ocras! Ocras!*" The wailing sounds like the keening at a wake, but no, it sounds more like animals crying in their near death when they have been mortally wounded. It's wailing that sounds like utter despair and desolation. Flashes of the flowers in the garden come to my memory as the fleshless, bony faces of these people appear before me. I crawl closer. As frightened as I am, I can't keep myself from them. I want to help. Then I see that they aren't human at all! My heart races with terror! They are some other creatures I have never seen before. They only resemble humans! I cry out with my own howl, a howl of terror when I see that they wear soft hair all over their faces and arms that looks like down on a goose. I stand up and begin to run away and back down the field and over the hill towards home. As I run, I hear a horse ride up behind me. The agent has come for me! I am suddenly scooped up and put upon his horse, held by angry and strong arms. All I can do is cling to him as he rides off with me, to what I think will become my death.

"Nora, where are you? Come, child, out of the dresser. We'll all be going to the O'Connors' field again to look for more potatoes," Mam says. Mam, Meg, and Kate have come in from outside and have been drying by the fire. I wake slowly from a death-like sleep. I haven't died! Did I only dream of the monsters I saw at the big house?

"Kate! Kate!" I cry out. Kate comes to me in the dresser and helps me climb out. I begin weeping in her arms as she tries to comfort me.

"I'm not dead, Kate, I'm not dead after all!"

"No, Nora, you're not to be dying on us, now. Meg and I can't do all the work, you know," Kate teases me.

Then I learn of my escape from the landlord's castle. It wasn't the agent who put me upon his horse. It had been Mr. Garvey, the landlord's coachman, who had been given the terrible job of riding off the beggars in the fields. He had seen me and recognized who I was, for he knew my Da. He brought me home and Kate told Mam to put me in the dresser to rest, for she knew it must have been a terrible experience.

"You'll not be going near the big house ever again, Nora!" Mam says firmly. "Do ya hear me, girl?" I nod quickly, wondering if Mam knew about the people lingering around the village who didn't look human.

"And you're getting too big to be crawling in the cupboard of a dresser, Nora," Mam says, untying her dirty apron and reaching for her shawl. I watch Mam as she drapes the beautiful red shawl over her head and around her shoulders. Mam has hair like Meg's even though it is now highlighted with white strands throughout it. She keeps it twisted around her face and knotted behind her head. I think Mam's face and figure are the perfect form of womanliness. She possesses a mixture of gentleness and strength that makes me think of ripeness. She possesses the colors of an apple orchard at harvest time, in spite of her harshness at times towards us.

"Come, Nora . . . Kate and Meg, too. We'll be needing to look for something to eat," Mam says. I have to wash my face and walk out the door with my Mam and sisters as if I had never seen the poor creatures at the landlord's.

Mrs. O'Connor and her children have been foraging throughout the countryside looking for something to eat from nature's storehouse just as we have been doing. Hadn't I just been in the field picking a few berries to eat? I wonder if life was ever going to be more than washing ourselves, looking for food, cooking our food, and eating our food. Will I ever have books to read and more learning to do?

"We paid the rent with the money from the Cake, Marion, and I gave my good shawl and my kettle to John to pawn them on his way to the Relief Works," Mrs. O'Connor says to Mam when we meet them at her cottage door.

"You can eat out of the same pot with us, then, Maeve. Put on a proper face now and let's go to your field and see if there are any more potatoes to squeeze the life out of," Mam says.

"I've enough cabbage leaves to cook my spuds in. I won't be missing my kettle for awhile," Mrs. O'Connor answers. We walk into the dying potato field.

I don't want to feel the stinking rot and mud in the garden between my toes again. I have had enough of it, and long to feel the grass on my feet and the smell of honeysuckle in my hair. Mam doesn't understand how I feel, and she doesn't know how weak from the hunger I really am, I think gloomily.

We have already found every last potato in our own field of potatoes. Mam said this would be our last attempt to find some healthy ones anywhere. Most of the neighbors have smaller fields than we have and Mam said it wouldn't be right asking them if we could look in their fields.

Eileen O'Connor, Kate, and I walk together into the muddy field. We wrap our shawls around our noses so we don't smell the dunglike scent of the rotting potatoes. We begin leaning over and picking through the plants, pulling up one potato after another. Each one turns into mush in our hands. We work for half an hour and don't find any healthy ones.

I can see Meg, Mam, and the rest of the O'Connors at the far end of the field. I untie my shawl and walk over to Eileen and Kate, suddenly feeling brave after my ordeal at the landlord's.

"I'm going to pretend to go for some water, but I'm really going to the other side of the stream to find some more berries to eat. Come along a little while after I go and we'll have a sport of it!" I say hopefully.

"No, Nora, 'tis wrong to leave everyone working so hard in this field," Kate replies.

"I'll go, Nora, I'll go," Eileen says cheerfully. Eileen is only nine and can be easily led astray.

"Kate, don't you see? We're wasting our time here in this rotten mess. If we go hunting for some berries and other things, we'll have some food that we find ourselves. I was out this morning looking for berries and know there's plenty to be found," I say.

"You're a convincing one, just like you talked Meg and Da into believing that exchanging Miss Maggie Hen for your comb was right, too," Kate replies.

At the mention of my hen, I drop my head, "Don't say the name of my favorite pet, Kate."

"I'm sorry, Nora. You go on ahead then, and we'll follow," Kate says.

"Thanks be to God!" cries Eileen, and one by one we sneak away from the field of stinking potatoes.

The stream is very high from all the rain. It gurgles and roars in my ears and makes me think it's laughing at all our troubles. As I watch it flowing furiously over the rocks, I know it'll be difficult to cross to the other side where I can see more bushes full of berries that the birds haven't found yet.

"And where do you think we should cross, Nora?" Kate asks. I can tell Kate doesn't think this is a good idea after all.

"Let's walk along the stream and find a place where the water isn't so strong," I say to her.

"Clear to Cork City are we to go?" Kate asks sarcastically.

"I can swim!" cries wee Eileen.

"You stay away from the water, Eileen, or you'll be swallowed by a big fish like Jonah was," I tell her sternly.

Eileen slumps down into the tall grass and begins picking the yellow cowslips that are bowed down by all the rain.

Kate follows me as I walk alongside the stream looking for a shallow place to cross. A few minutes later, we hear Eileen's voice crying in the distance. When we look back, we see that Eileen has fallen into the water and is being carried by its violent force down towards where we stand.

"I can't bear to look!" I cry out, my fear closing in on me and preventing me from rescuing Eileen. I turn to run for help and Kate begins running alongside the creek as Eileen floats by. Then Eileen's dress gets caught on a rock and it holds her in place.

"Nora!" Kate yells. "Help me free her from the rock!"

I run back and reach for Eileen across the stream. She is choking and gagging on the water that is spilling over her face.

"Give me your hand, Eileen, give me your hand!" I scream at her.

Kate holds on to me with one arm, and with the other arm I pull Eileen onto the bank. Her dress is torn and most of it is in the stream attached to the rock. Eileen is sobbing and her legs and arms are bleeding from scratches made by the rocks.

"My dress! My dress is nearly gone from me!" she cries.

Kate and I bring Eileen back to the O'Connors' hearth. We dry her off, apply some crushed lavender to her cuts, and wrap her in a shawl. Then we walk into the field where the rest of our families are still hunting for potatoes.

"Mrs. O'Connor," I say, when she is bent over and digging in the ground, "I've done a terrible deed." I decide to blurt it out all at once and get it over with, but a sharp pain attacks my stomach. My hunger pains have become worse. As I look at the ground, I see a small potato that doesn't look blackened. I reach for it, wipe it off on my apron, and stuff it into my mouth.

I immediately gag and spit it out, for inside the potato lies the sinister disease. I cough and become sick in front of Mrs. O'Connor.

Mrs. O'Connor pulls me to her side. "And don't I know that there could be no terrible deed worse than the pestilence that has come upon us. Be still, pet, and tell me what it is you have done."

"Kate, Eileen, and I left the field and went to pick berries," I tell her. "Eileen fell into the stream and cut herself, but she's grand now and resting by the hearth. It's her dress that isn't grand, for it was torn from her when it caught on a rock. And it's not her fault, it's all mine . . . "

Mrs. O'Connor starts for the cottage and I follow her. "Stay away in the field, Nora, you've done enough damage today. My Eileen has no other piece of clothing to put on her wee body."

I find my Mam and the others in the field. I confess to her what I have done.

"Away from me, my Nora, for sometimes you're a wicked child. You'll need to be punished, but go . . . go away from me, and mind, no dawdling," Mam says angrily, waving her arms wildly at me.

I know my Mam will forget to punish me because she's too concerned with finding food for the lot of us. It makes me feel worse that I won't be punished. It makes it all the more real that our lives aren't normal. As I begin to go into the cottage, another sharp pain comes upon me and I fall to the ground gripping my belly.

"This is my punishment!" I lie on the grass crying until Kate and Meg help me into the cottage.

After I am warmed and have eaten a turnip that has been found in the O'Connors' garden and roasted over the turf fire, I climb into the dresser. Mam and my sisters sit around the hearth with some mending, trying not to think about tomorrow. Mam tells us that Jesus said not to worry about tomorrow, as tomorrow takes care of itself, and that we need to be looking at the birds of the field and the flowers of the field. The angels will take care of us, Mam says, for each child has a special one.

As I think about what my angel might look like, I remember my wee little friend, Eileen, without a bit of clothing to wear, all because of me! Then a whispering wind blows through the cottage, into the dresser, and into my heart. I quickly crawl out of the cupboard and go to the straw bedding where we keep our clothing wrapped and folded as neatly as possible. I unfold my fancy dress, smooth the creases out of it the best I can, and notice a button is missing. I ask Mam for a spare one. Mam shakes her head, claiming she has only a few left, but then she gives me one anyway. The button is the perfect size, though a different color than the rest. I sew it to the dress and then fold the dress carefully. I wrap my shawl around my shoulders, and hide the dress underneath it.

"I must visit the O'Connors, Mam," I say.

Mam looks up from her mending, puzzled by my statement. "It's not fit for a child to be out, Nora. I have heard that many people have taken to the roads to look for food. They're despairing and will do anything to find food to eat," Mam says, the worry in her face causing her to appear much older than she is. I then remember the starving creatures at the landlord's, and a chill goes through me.

"It's not yet dark and I know the way well, Mam," I answer.

"I'll go with Nora," Kate says, looking up from beside the hearth.

"And what, in the name of God and His Mother, do you need to be going there for, child?" Mam asks.

"I've got to be helping Eileen, Mam, for she's naked without a dress because of my foolishness," I answer.

"Away then, pet. God's blessing on both of you, and hurry home before the evening prayers."

We walk the same quiet, narrow road we had traveled on early in the morning, but it was now a scene to break our hearts.

"It's Da!" I cry out when I see two men slowly meandering down the road before us. I run ahead of Kate and when I get close to the men, I stop and cover my mouth in fright, and turn to wait for Kate.

"Don't run, child, don't be afraid. All of this will pass! The luck that is not on us today may be on us tomorrow," one of the frail-looking men says to me as he and the other man approach Kate and me. I seem to freeze in place and I can't move my feet. Kate soon catches up with me. Kate's face is filled with the same terror I feel within my beating chest. We move to the side of the road and the two men greet us by tipping their worn-out top hats with the brims hanging half off.

We watch as the men, pale and gaunt, their eyes mad and empty, and their gait feeble, totter down the road, barely able to walk. Their garments are like our Da's that he hates to wear—coarse frieze coats as decrepit as they appear to be themselves, bare elbows showing through in one, and the other sewn with patches.

"God help us, Nora, we're all poor in Ireland," Kate says, trying to comfort me.

"But never did I see bones walking in coats," I answer.

"Let's be on our way before it gets too late," Kate says, and though we are weakened from not enough food, we run the rest of the way to the O'Connors' cottage.

Mrs. O'Connor cries out when she hears us knock on her door, "We've nothing in the kettle, and not even a kettle do we own now. Away from us, for we have nothing here to eat!" Mrs. O'Connor thinks that we are starving people traveling on the roads.

"It's Nora and Kate," I say.

The door opens and Kate and I are warmly invited in for a sup of tea. We stand awkwardly before the four O'Connor children and their mother, who have been sitting around their hearth saying the evening prayers.

"I've something for Eileen," I say, as I pull my fancy dress out from under my shawl. I hand it to Eileen, who is in her petticoat and wrapped in a bright blue shawl. She quickly drops her shawl to the floor to put on the dress I've brought her. I am shocked to see how thin Eileen has become. The dress is too large for her but it covers her wee body and makes her smile.

"Thanks be to God," Mrs. O'Connor says, "I can take it in to make it fit her properly, Nora." Then she thinks a minute and turns to me. "No, Nora, this is your own. Is it your fancy dress, girl?"

"No matter, Mrs. O'Connor, for I'm wearing a dress now and it is lovely for fancy times or working with my Mam. Da will be home soon and I'll have another one, the Lord be praised."

Mrs. O'Connor walks over to me and hugs me to her skirts. "Yes, praise be to God, my John and your own Da will be home soon. The seed potatoes will bring another harvest and we'll have some grain to carry us through. Oh my pets, it might be that they'll bring us some meat and a hen or two!"

The O'Connor children get up from sitting around the hearth and begin jumping for joy, Padraic proclaiming, "Another Cake, Mam, another Cake we'll be having!"

"And dancing, too . . . like this," Eileen says, and she grabs Kate's and my hands to form a circle to dance. We circle once but feel too weak for play and sit down again, but hope is stirring in our childish hearts.

Kate and I take our leave from the O'Connors' cottage and make our way home without seeing anyone walking like skeletons with a bit of skin on them. Our prayers that evening around the hearth seem to sing like joyous melodies. It is then I decide to sleep in the dresser until all will be right in Ireland, for it is in the dresser where I find hope.

Chapter Five

BOXTY CAKES, CORNMEAL, AND A MAGIC COW

"Hold it, hold it and squeeze, Nora!" Mam instructs me.

"It stinks, Mam!" I press the pulp from the potato into a cloth and watch in horror as grayish black liquid emerges.

"This one is rotten to the core," I say, as I shake loose the rot from the cloth and rinse it in a pail of water.

Mam and I try to scrape each of the eight healthy potatoes we found in the O'Connors' field. At least they look good on the outside. We try to squeeze all the pulp out of them that isn't putrid. We then place the pulp in a cloth, squeeze each one as dry as possible, and flatten them into cakes.

"These are boxty cakes, Nora, and they'll save us from the hunger. Go, call your sisters to come in and we'll have us some new spuds," Mam says.

I go to look for my sisters, but I'm dreaming of food as I skip out to the fields. Meg and Kate are out gathering gooseberries they found earlier in the day. I have the feeling Mam wants to keep me by her side so I won't get into any more trouble.

I'm so excited about the boxty cakes, I could dance a jig! My mouth waters just thinking about spreading them with tangy mustard and popping one, two, and maybe three into my mouth!

46

Then I see Kate and Meg running with a pail half full of gooseberries towards me. What a feast we'll be having together. If only I wasn't pining for Miss Maggie Hen and Da. I want them to be sitting around the hearth just like it was before the pestilence came upon us. How long ago was it, I wonder, when Da played the fiddle after our evening meal and prayers, and a neighbor came to do some storytelling?

Later, Mam bakes the boxty cakes on tongs over the red coals on the hearth. When one side is done, she turns the cake until almost all the liquid evaporates and the cake is as hard and dry as a crust of bread. I eat two cakes and imagine the hearty food traveling to every part of my body, giving me strength.

I reach for another one off the hearth but Mam stops me. "No, Nora, save one for tomorrow morning when you'll be feeling the hunger again. By tomorrow's end, I hope we'll see your Da come walking in here with something else for us to eat," Mam says sadly.

The cottage is swept and tidied, and the evening prayers are said. Everyone scrambles to bed and I climb into the dresser. As I am falling to sleep, I remember the poem Da taught me:

There shall be peace and plenty—the
kindly open door, Blessings on all who come
and go—the prosperous or the poor. The misty
glens and purple hills a fairer tint shall show,
When your splendid Sun shall ride the skies
again—*Mo Chraoibhin Cno!*
(My brown-eyed girl, My Ireland!)

All the next day we keep waiting for Da's return but he doesn't come. I am busy mashing the gooseberries for jam, although there is no more sugar to make it sweet. The strawberry jam has been eaten long ago. Meg, Kate, and Mam keep themselves busy mending and cleaning the cottage. There have been people outside our door early in the morning begging for food. I know it breaks Mam's heart to turn them away, but we have nothing to eat but berries and one boxty cake each. Mam has placed the butter churn and the stool up against the door in order to prevent anyone from coming in if they become desperate enough. It makes me tremble to think someone might come into our home and hurt us.

Meg yells at me for the third time because I have licked jam with my fingers. I yell back and then hear the clatter of horses' hooves come up the lane. We all run to the window to look out. It's Father O'Boyle and another man from our parish.

Mam moves the furniture away from the door and opens it to greet our priest and his companion. Father O'Boyle is mighty thin looking, and I wonder if he, too, is feeling the hunger we are all feeling. It makes me uneasy to think the priest himself is suffering like we all are.

"I've brought some grain to help you until Eoin returns from the Works," Father O'Boyle says, as he sets down a small burlap bag.

We crowd around the bag, our mouths already watering, thinking it might be oatmeal and there will be oatmeal cakes to eat. "Maybe Mrs. O'Connor will have some cabbage leaves to go with them," I think.

"But God help us all, Maeve, this grain is not anything we Irish are used to feeding our bellies. It's cornmeal from America and it'll take some getting used to," Father O'Boyle says.

I can't believe my ears to think that someone in America knows of our suffering and is helping us. "God be praised!" I say, quietly.

"It's grand, Father, really grand! May God's blessings be with you. I'm waiting for my Eoin to come walking in the door any time now, God willing," Mam says to Father O'Boyle.

"I'll be going. I've many deliveries yet to make. May God and His Son bless and keep you all," Father

O'Boyle says, as he leaves us staring at the bag of strange meal. We shut the door and prop the furniture back up against it again. We can hardly believe there is a big bag of food sitting before us. We rip it open so quickly that some of the cornmeal flies out and covers my face.

"You look like a ghost, Nora!" Kate laughs.

"Don't you waste a pinch of it, Nora!" Mam yells, and she makes me stand over the bag and shake my head so that any of the meal on my face will drop back into the bag. I shake my head but tears begin flowing because I'm longing for Da and I'm always getting into trouble. When I look up from the bag, there are two long streaks of dried cornmeal running down my face. Everyone, even Mam, laughs to see my funny face. I laugh, too, for I can imagine how hilarious I must look.

Mam doesn't quite know how to cook the new grain from America, but she's certain it isn't much different from any other grain she's used in her cooking. She goes about mixing it with some water first and then places it over the fire. She adds a pinch of salt and then we wait for it to boil and cook.

"The buttermilk would taste well with it, but we haven't had any since the O'Connor cow went to her death off the cliff," Meg says longingly.

After the cornmeal has cooked for a few minutes, we spoon it out into wooden bowls and begin eating it. We gag, for it tastes like strange and bitter mush, very bland and gritty. I can't help myself and spit some out on the floor.

"Shame on you, Nora, for this is not to be wasted. It's food from America, and food from America is as good as gold," Mam says with tears in her eyes.

We are so hungry that we choke down the cornmeal mush, this gold from America. What is wrong with this country that sends us bitter-tasting grain, this land across the sea we're supposed to go to if Da ever comes home for us?

I cry myself to sleep in the dresser after our bitter-tasting meal and evening prayers. Da has not come home and my belly is big and bloated after eating so much of this new grain. I wonder what we will eat next, for Mam says that the new food from America is not to be eaten like there's no tomorrow. Will there be a tomorrow? All of us feel so ill, there are moans coming from us as we try to sleep. I touch Da's fiddle and whisper in a prayer, "Please, God, bring my Da home to us soon."

We hear someone at our door early the next morning. I am the first one to peek out the window to see who it is, hoping it is our Da. It's Mrs. O'Connor, Padraic, Eileen, and the younger children. The door is opened and the O'Connors all come in looking worried, even though Eileen dances around me showing off the dress that I had given her.

"My youngest, Michael, is sick, Maeve. The food Father O'Boyle brought to us is poisoning the lot of us. It's a cruel trick the English and the Americans have done to try and to kill us all," Mrs. O'Connor cries, "and then they can be rid of the likes of us papists forever!" She sinks down to the floor by the hearth, her children clinging to her. They all begin whimpering.

"We'll not be perishing, Maeve. We've all been ill from this strange food we've eaten, but the priest has blessed it and given it to us when we were starving. We've had very little in our bellies and they're not used to the likes of this grain," Mam says to poor Mrs. O'Connor. "It'll take time for our bellies to adjust to it."

"Go, Meg, see if you can find some leaves to make some peppermint tea for all of us," Mam says.

"I'll go, too," I say, eager to be out doing something to help. I have begun to feel the weight of sadness pressing in on me. I'm frightened to see a grown woman cry and become so weak before her children. I've never seen it before, except when a woman is giving birth to her baby.

Meg and I walk in different directions once we leave our cottage. The rain has stopped, but there is no sight of the sun to brighten our hard days.

"The sun would only mock us to shine upon us now in our hardship," I say to myself.

I walk into the countryside, which appears green and lush from all the rain. My eyes fill with the sight of large clumps of bracken and gorse everywhere, the gorse with its colorful yellow petals that seem to brighten the fields and hillsides.

"No need for the sun then, for its rays must have fallen to the ground and stayed!" I exclaim as I drink in the beauty surrounding me. I keep walking, as if I'm in a trance, taken up from my earthly sorrows by this carpeted field of gorse and other wild flowers. The clover is so green, it doesn't look real. I am feverish as I begin looking for a four-leaf clover, forgetting about all my troubles. I know it's considered great luck to find one, especially when the hunger is upon us.

"I will bring one home and place it in Da's fiddle," I think to myself as I hunt in the grass.

I hear chirping of wrens and the coos of a woodpigeon. They sing songs of joy that take away my heavy sadness. I keep walking until I come to a hedgerow overgrown with hawthorn and nettles. Suddenly, I see a brown hare scamper through the rocks. It startles me, for I have heard that old women with supernatural powers turn themselves into hares to steal milk from other people's cows. I make the sign of the cross and walk along the edge of the hedgerow away from where I saw the hare.

Then I remember I'm supposed to be looking for peppermint leaves for tea to take away the sickness we all feel in our bellies from the grain we've eaten that came from America. As I look around the hedgerow wall, I see an opening and peer through. I can't believe my eyes! There is a cow standing on the other side of the hedgerow all alone and as big and beautiful as I have ever seen. Then I remember the hare I had just seen. Perhaps it is going to turn into an old woman and steal some milk from the cow, this cow I have found!

"I must get to it before the hare does!" I exclaim, as I look for an opening in the wall of the hedgerow to climb through. I decide to climb over the wall, and as I struggle to pull myself over, I become entangled in all kinds of brush, nettles, and hawthorn needles. I cry out in pain but keep climbing until I have gotten over the hedgerow. I creep slowly to the cow, talking in a sweet high-pitched tone, "There, Miss Pretty Cow, don't be afraid of me, my pet, for I'll be your friend." The cow looks into my eyes and lows as if to say, "I've been waiting all day for you to come!"

I look around the field but don't see any other animals or even a farm from where the cow might have come. There's no mark on the animal to determine who it belongs to. Maybe it's lost, and someone will be looking for her. Oh, but maybe it has been sent to me by God to take back to my family. I stroke the animal on its back and she seems content to have me touch her.

"Do you want to come home with me, Miss Pretty?" I ask her as I begin walking along the edge of the hedgerow looking for a low place to pull the cow over. I don't have to force the cow to come with a switch, for she is eager to follow behind me. I'm delighted with my new friend, a gift from the fairies that God has sent me. The cow and I walk a mile along the hedgerow until we find a place in the wall where there's an opening. We're able to walk through to the other side and then I retrace my steps back to where I first crawled over. Soon, the cow and I make our way home to the cottage. I can see the smoke coming out of the cottage and the children playing and looking for food in the field. I know that they are rooting in the ground for chickweed, sorrel, and pignuts to add to the dreadful cornmeal. I begin walking faster, eager to introduce my magic cow to my family and the O'Connors. "Now we will have plenty of milk to mix with our American gold," I think excitedly.

"Look at Nora!" Padraic says, and he and the children run to me as I walk to the front of the cottage with the lowing cow. Mam and Mrs. O'Connor come out of the cottage and stand before me and Miss Pretty.

"Oh no, Nora, for the love of God, you shouldn't have done this!" Mam cries. "You'll be sending us all to prison!" Mam brings up her apron over her face and I'm immediately ashamed for what I've done.

Meg comes to me and takes me by my shoulders and shakes me. "You wicked child, Nora, to steal an animal from someone's field!"

I'm surprised and hurt that no one thinks the cow is a miracle! Don't they realize I have been at the right place at the right time to find a magic cow? I stumble over my words and begin crying, "I found her, I did, I found her, Mam. She was all alone in a field and no one was around!" I run past everyone standing before me, into the cottage, and right into the dresser where I cry even harder.

Mrs. O'Connor walks over to Mam and says, "Let's tie the cow up, Marion, until we can decide what to do. She means well, you know that. You know Nora always means well. She's just a child."

"And I suppose she's gone and named the animal as well," Meg says as she finds a rope to tie the cow to a post.

"Go children, go back out to the field and leave us be," Mam says to the little ones standing around large-eyed and confused.

"I'll go to Nora, Mam," Kate says, and then she comes into the cottage to find me in the dresser. I've heard everything they're saying about me, but I know Mam doesn't believe Mrs. O'Connor that I mean well in everything I do. She won't ever believe it!

"Come out, Nora. It's me, Kate."

"No, Kate, it's no use. I never do anything right. Everything I do comes to no good!"

Kate opens the cupboard door and reaches in to rub my back as I sob.

"Never mind, Nora. It will be alright. I think your cow is a magic cow and none of us will be going to prison."

The next day, Mrs. O'Connor and Mam pay a visit to Father O'Boyle to ask him for his help concerning the cow I've found. Meg watches the children like a hawk, making them look for food surrounding the cottage. There is little to eat and we've all been combing through the fields day after day. Only the grain from America is left for us to try and swallow. We're all very hungry and the wee ones burst into tears from time to time. The cow has been given some water and a place to graze in the grass. No one dares go near it or even look at it. We've all heard tales of a person stealing a piece of bread and then being put on a ship to Australia, a faraway land where there are no homes or food. I was certain I'd be going there for stealing a cow!

When Mam and Mrs. O'Connor return, the children notice they have a stranger with them. He's an old, frail-looking man, bent over and tattered in his coat with tails and top hat falling apart. I look closely at him and realize it is one of the men who spoke to Kate and me the other day on the road to the O'Connors' cottage. He spoke strange words of hope but he looked like walking death!

The three of them walk over to the cow and the children all gather around to see what is going to happen. Then Mam says, "Father O'Boyle will get the message out that we found someone's cow, for the wandering cow was in a field not belonging to a farmer. This kindly man, Mr. Collins, was nearby when I spoke to the priest. He's offered to help us bleed the cow without hurting her so that we might benefit from her until her owner is found. The bleeding will nourish us more than the milk, which might not be enough anyway for she's been alone in a field and has probably not been milked in a long time." Mam is shaking and I think that she must be weak from the hunger, or maybe she is afraid of killing the cow that isn't hers. Mr. Collins looks at me strangely, "I met you and your sister on the road the other day. Did I not tell you that weeping might endure for a night but joy comes in the morning?"

"Yes, sir, you did," I answer. I'm surprised to see someone so frail and thin able to speak so grand. I cock my head to look at him and notice the gleam in his eyes.

The cow lows at the old man and they seem to know each other. Da told me that during hard times in Ireland, certain farmers with a reputation for being able to bleed an animal to extract its blood for nourishment are in great demand. If an animal isn't bled correctly, it can bleed to death. The blood is mixed with grain and becomes a fortifier to our diet. It can sustain us and keep us alive even when the pestilence visits our potato crops. When the people are starving, it is a miracle to behold food being made right before their eyes. I'm thinking I'll be ill if I look at the cow being bled and turn my head away, but then I turn around to watch. I can't help myself. I have to see if Miss Pretty will be okay.

Mr. Collins takes a knife out of his pocket and tells us to get a bucket. When Meg hands him a pail, he gets ready with his knife.

"Her name is Miss Pretty," I say, "so please don't hurt her."

"Well, Miss Pretty, you'll be giving us some of your wealth today," Mr. Collins says as he cuts a vein in the neck of the cow and begins to control the flow of blood by exerting pressure against the vein with his finger. The cow lets out one moan and looks at me quizzically. My breath catches in my throat but my belly growls to think there will be something nourishing to eat later. I'm so hungry, even the thought of drinking blood does not sicken me or anyone standing around watching this strange procedure. I think that the hunger must be making us all crazy in Ireland.

When the blood reaches a certain level in the bucket, Mr. Collins stops the flow by slipping a pin through the skin across the incision in the vein and tying it securely in place with a few hairs he has cut from the cow's tail.

Everyone cheers and Mr. Collins is invited in for a sup of tea and to partake of the cornmeal mixed with the blood and baked in some of Mrs. O'Connor's cabbage leaves. After the meal and our evening prayers, Mr. Collins begins telling stories, and along with the hearty meal we've had, we forget that the hunger is upon us again in Ireland. When I climb into the dresser to sleep that night, and Mr. Collins has gone, I think I hear the cow low in such a way it sounds like a sad, but beautiful, song.

The next day the cow disappeared! We look all around the fields and Mam visits the priest again and asks for Mr. Collins. He is gone and it is firmly believed that a miracle has come to us. There is enough blood for two days and there is no danger of being accused of stealing the cow. I am so pleased to think that I was the one who stumbled upon Miss Pretty all on my own.

Chapter Six

FATHER

"Da!" He's come home and I cling to him when he walks through the door three days after the magic cow has disappeared. I feel how thin and bony he has become as I hug his waist. How can this be the same strong man I have been frightened of when I disobeyed? His clothes are tattered, dirty, and falling off him, with the uncomfortable swallowtail coattails ripped and tied around his waist.

"Eoin McCabe, you've come home to feed us!" Mam says, as she goes to Da. Kate and Meg also run to him and we all embrace for a long time in the doorway. Then we collapse by the hearth from exhaustion and hunger. It is almost worse to have the blood from the cow for a few days because it has whet our appetites for nourishment, and left our bodies remembering what it now can't have. I had been rooting furiously behind the cottage for something to eat just before Da returned home. Da has not eaten anything but wild onions and some berries on his long walk home from the Relief Works.

"God have mercy, Marion," he says, while we are attentive and hang on to every word. "At first I was unable to work because they're not hiring anyone who has a quarter acre of land or more. Only those evicted from their homes for not being able to pay their rent are being hired to do the meaningless work building roads for the English." Da puts his head down for a moment, and then continues, "The evicted tenants are living in hovels built in the hillsides and they're weak from the hunger. Still, they keep working on the roads—men and women dying from this hunger that has come again. We are like the Israelite slaves of the Egyptians! Will God part the sea for us, Marion?"

I have never seen my father so sad, the flesh on his face hanging with gloom. Even when our potato crops have failed in the past and there was scarcity, Da never was without hope for all of us. Mam clasps Da's hands to her breast,

"But Eoin, did you find work? What is in the bags you've brought us?"

"Our neighbor, O'Connor, and I were fortunate enough to be given the names of two dead men by some people traveling on the road to the Relief Works. We took their names for our own, God have mercy on their souls, for they had been evicted, got the fever, and died. We worked on the roads for some gruel and very little wages to buy the grain I've brought home. Then I heard the landlord had once again gone back to England and was planning on evicting those of us who cannot pay the rent next month. So I left the Works to come home."

"Blessed Jesus, Eoin, you have enough from the wages for the rent then!" Mam says.

Meg, Kate, and I opened the bags of oats and cornmeal that Da has lugged into the cottage. We begin making some oaten cakes over the hearth, our stomachs growling and our ears listening to every word Da speaks.

I look at his face and it seems to droop to his chest. I want to go to him and caress it back into the shape of the father I have always known. How can this be the same man who had a twinkle in his eye at the O'Connors' Cake, my soft-hearted Da who didn't punish me for hiding Miss Maggie Hen!

After we have eaten our first meal in two days, our hunger has been satisfied but our bodies aren't used to so much food all at once. We feel ill, but all agree that it's a feeling worth having as it isn't as severe as the hunger pains.

"Da," I say, hoping to bring back some gladness to my father, "I've a surprise for you."

I open the cupboard of the dresser and bring out his fiddle and bow. For a moment, I'm uncertain whether Da is pleased, for he just stares blankly at me, holding the fiddle. Then he smiles and I remember this smile almost like his old one. I think that there is nothing like old smiles and I'd rather have old smiles than new strange ones like the one from the old man who bled the magic cow.

Da takes the fiddle in his hands, rubs the wood on it for a long time, and with his bony fingers begins playing and singing a melancholy tune, "The Heart is True":

Our ship is ready to bear away.
Come, comrades, o'er the stormy sea.
Her snow white wings they are unfurled
And soon she'll swim in a watery world.

Ah, do not forget, love, do not grieve
The heart is true and can't deceive.
My heart and hand with you I'll leave
Fare thee well, true love, remember me.

Da finishes the tune and everyone in the cottage is quiet, sitting with their heads bowed, as if in prayer. He puts his fiddle down and stares into the fire. I can't bear to listen to the tension in the silence that has blanketed our cottage.

"Da, why did you play that tune?" I ask.

He turns away from the fire and gathers all of us together with his eyes. "The great Atlantic will become the Red Sea for the McCabes, as it will part for us so we can travel to America. We'll not lament it, for it will be the saving of our lives." Mam utters a scream and covers her mouth, and my sisters and I begin bombarding our father with questions about America.

Later, I curl up in the dresser and try to sleep. My mind is filled with thoughts about America. It has been said that New York is a big city full of rich foods, clothing, and opportunities. I have heard people say the streets are paved with gold, but because they said it with laughter in their eyes, I have never believed it. I can imagine the luxurious food I'll be eating, like pie and grand cakes that are better than potatoes and buttermilk. My belly churns and my mouth waters thinking about it, even though I have eaten three oaten cakes for the evening meal.

During the month after Da returned to us, I have had sleepless nights imagining the fancy desserts, dresses, jewels, and ribbons that will be in America. Mam says there will be soft furniture to sit in just like at the landlord's big house. But after seeing all these visions of America, my mind is always jolted back to where I am now—Ireland. How can I leave this magical green land that is home to so many different kinds of birds like the cuckoo, skylarks, puffins, and jays? What about the storytellers who come for a sup of tea around the hearth and the music my Da and his friends play together? Will they play fiddles and sit around the hearth and listen to one another's thoughts in America? "God help me," I think as I try to fall asleep each evening, "I want both! I want to stay in Ireland and I want to go to America!"

Chapter Seven

THE TUMBLING

We are all awakened by a loud pounding on the door early in the morning before the birds have sung their first praises. My heart beats as fast as a galloping horse as I imagine it must be someone who has come to take our new grain away! I heard Mam and Da talking as they sat around the hearth last night, and they said people in the village are committing all kinds of crimes to get some food for their hungry bellies. I scramble out of the dresser and can see everyone is waking up because of the noise. Da tells us all to hush.

"Who is there?" he cries out.

"It's Maeve, your neighbor, Eoin! Please open!"

Da opens the door to Maeve O'Connor, who stands alone. It's the first time I ever remember seeing her without her wee ones surrounding her skirts. Mam comes to the door and pulls her inside, telling Meg to start a fire and prepare the tea. I notice Mrs. O'Connor's hands are trembling and she isn't wearing a shawl. I wonder sadly if she has sold it in the market so she could buy food for her family.

"Sit on the stool, Maeve," Mam says as she helps her friend sit down. It is plain to see that she is distraught and Meg, Kate, and I are staring at her. Mam is displeased by our behavior, thinking it is disrespectful. "Away out of here, girls!" Mam says angrily. Mrs. O'Connor puts her face in her hands and Mam holds her while she weeps. Da sits on the other side of her. After the tea is made, Meg, Kate, and I busy ourselves tidying up the cottage, fearful Mam will make us leave the cottage. We don't want to miss a word that is said.

"We have to leave our home!" Mrs. O'Connor cries out. "They'll be coming to tumble our home any hour now! We've paid half our rent on Gale Day, but the agent came last eve telling us he'd come today with the constable for the rest of the money, and if he didn't get it, he'd be tearing down our walls!"

"Then you'll be comin' here to us for shelter, Maeve," Mam says. I'm glad for Mam's compassion, but I try not to imagine what it'll be like having five more people living in our small cottage.

"Are you mad, Marion? The O'Boyles' cottage was tumbled and they went to stay with their kin and then their cottage was torn down as well! It is the same punishment for anyone who takes an evicted family into their home."

"We'll stop the greedy hounds from tearing you down, Maeve!" Da exclaims.

"Have you any wages left over from the Works, Eoin?" Mrs. O'Connor asks. I can see in her face that she feels ashamed to be asking.

"Maeve, I'd give you any extra I had, but we paid only half our rent to get us through until we go to America. I've only money saved for our tickets. But you can be living here, caring for our home! We're good on the rent for a few months. And we'll be handing over our cottage to you, right and legal."

"There Maeve," Mam says. "Eoin is right. You can be staying here."

Mrs. O'Connor throws her arms up in the air and screams, "Are you daft, McCabes? This cottage, too, will be tumbled if you house a family whose own home has gone down!" Maeve O'Connor threw down her teacup and ran out of our cottage. I stand gaping at the broken cup, for I know that it's an omen that something dreadful will happen this day.

"Clean up the cottage, girls!" Da shouts, "I'm going over to wake Maeve's poor husband who probably doesn't know his wife's mind has become unstable."

After Da leaves and Mam and my sisters begin preparing some oaten cakes for our breakfast, I quietly slip outside. The morning dew glistens on the grass next to our cottage door from the sun's attempt to rise on our part of the world. I wonder why it sparkles like diamonds as if nothing is wrong. Then I remember what old Mags from the village told us one day after Mass, "Wash your face in the morning dew if you want to be beautiful and your hands in it if you want to be dexterous." I lie down in it, then, and begin to roll in its wet sparkles, making sure it gets all over my head, for I'm thinking my plain hair might turn to gold like Meg's hair.

"On my sorrow, I don't know what to do with you, Nora!" Mam says as she opens the half door and finds me slithering in the dew like a snake.

We wait anxiously for Da to return from the O'Connors'. I can tell Mam is nervous because she paces in front of the cottage, looking towards the road. In the afternoon, she tells us to stay inside and not allow anyone in. She leaves to look for Da at the O'Connors'. I climb into the dresser and try to pray every prayer and recite every blessing I know. I know the omen of the teacup is taking place. Kate tries to get me to play a game with her by the hearth, but I can't concentrate on anything but what might be going on at the O'Connors'. After awhile, I climb out of the dresser with purpose burning in my mind.

"I'm making my way to look for Mam and Da," I state to my sisters.

"You'll be doing no such thing, Nora," Meg says sternly.

"You're not my mammy, Meg. I'm going." I grab my shawl from our corner where we sleep and start for the door.

Meg gets off the stool and reaches for me. My shawl comes off in her hands. "If you really cared for Mam and Da, you'd be going, too!" I yell.

Kate comes to my side, "I'm going with Nora, Meg, and you'd best not be trying to stop us," she says calmly.

Meg gives me back my shawl and I wrap it around my shoulders as Kate and I walk out the door and leave Meg alone in the cottage.

I have never seen a cottage "tumbled" or torn down. An Irish cottage is a castle for the poor that sometimes has not only housed one family but their grandparents and great-grandparents before them. Tearing down the cottage is like tearing out the heart of the people.

When Kate and I arrive at the O'Connors', Da and Mr. O'Connor stand up from their stools around the hearth when we walk in without knocking. Mam and Mrs. O'Connor are preparing oaten cakes to take with them if the O'Connors have to leave their home and travel to another village. The children are nowhere to be seen. They must have been taken to a neighbor in hopes of shielding them from what is to come.

"Away with you, to home you go, girls!" Da shouts at Kate and me.

"This be no place for ye now!" shouts Mam.

"We want to stay and help you!" I shout back.

"Crazed hungry ones are killin' each other for the blackberries that aren't yet ripened, and you're running through the countryside to get yourself killed!" Mam shouts again. "There's no help you can give us here, Nora!"

"Home, go home, go home!" Da screams at me as never have I heard him do before.

Kate and I run out the door and half-way across the field instead of taking to the road. We don't know where we're going. We just keep running, for we're frightened over the change in Mam and Da, and the look of horror in all of their faces when we entered the cottage. They are waiting for something terrible to happen and I cannot go home and let it happen without me doing something about it.

"I'm frightened, Nora, I'm so frightened," Kate says while trying to get her breathing back to normal. We have stopped running and sit down in the field to watch the O'Connors' cottage.

"Is there a pitch fork near the hay shed, do you know, Kate?" I ask.

"There's probably one in the garden," Kate answers.

"We'll crawl to the hay shed and hide in it."

"It's so small. How can we hide under the hay without being seen?"

"Let's go," I say, and we begin walking towards the O'Connor cottage. When we get close to the edge of the field, we crawl and then sprint to the hay shed. There are mounds of hay and some corn sheaths lying about. Kate and I try to bury ourselves in the musty and damp hay, but first we find a pitch fork. I lay it beside me and burrow deep into the hay. Suddenly, I begin to shake and can't stop. Kate reaches for my hand.

"I can't save Da and Mam!" I whimper. "I don't know what to do with this pitch fork!"

"Pray, Nora, pray!" Kate whispers, and we begin reciting our prayers quietly. I keep shaking but try to keep what might happen to everyone out of my head. Much time passes until we are startled by the landlord's agent who rides up to the O'Connors' cottage. He alone is enough to terrorize my being, but he isn't alone. Redcoat soldiers and the sheriff have come, too. They ride up to the cottage door and yell for the O'Connors to come out. Mr. O'Connor walks out alone, shutting the door behind him. My heart feels as if it will burst through my dress. I wonder if it will become so tired, it will stop and then I will die.

"We want possession of this place. You had better clear out," the agent states angrily. "You didn't bring me the rent this morning."

Mr. O'Connor stands solemnly before the crowd of enemies outside his cottage. I can see that he is unable to speak.

"Get to work and clear everything out of your home, or everything in it will burn when the cottage is torn down," the constable says.

"*O maise, Dia linn* (God bless us)," was all Mr. O'Connor could manage to utter. He walks back inside the cottage and shuts the door. We see the constable whisper something to the agent. The redcoat soldiers walk their horses in closer to the cottage.

"I am giving you five minutes and no more to begin clearing everything out!" the constable commands in a loud voice. I reach for the pitch fork and one of the soldiers sees my movement in the hay. He speaks to the constable and then walks his horse closer to the hay shed. My arm is sticking out of the hay holding on to the fork.

"Come out of there or I'll shoot!" commands the soldier. I immediately stand to my feet, still holding the fork. Kate jumps up to my side. We are both breathing heavily as I raise the fork in the air towards the soldier.

"Don't lay a hand on us, sir!" I yell. The soldier laughs to see two children trying to defy him. He reaches down for the fork.

"Hand it to me carefully," he says, smiling. I'm ashamed to be so afraid and let him take it from me.

"Now sit down and don't move," he says. We sit back down in the hay shed, feeling defeated.

"Clear out, now, or we come in!" yells the constable towards the cottage.

The door opens and the O'Connors and Mam and Da walk out looking angry and conquered. They drag the few pieces of furniture the O'Connors own out of the cottage. The butter churn that had held the lovely cake on it just a few months before is pulled out by Mam. Slowly they work carrying out the furniture, not even looking at us in the hay shed. I don't think they see us, for they are sorrowing and determined to save what little furniture there is. Mrs. O'Connor is weeping and Mam is trying to console her while they empty the cottage.

"Stand back!" shouts the constable after everything is out. He nods to the soldier who has taken the pitch fork from me. The soldier walks into the cottage where some oaten cakes are still cooking on the hearth. He picks up a shovel of hot turf and walks outside with it. He hands it to another soldier to hold while he climbs back on his horse. Then he takes the shovel and carefully places the smoldering turf on top of the thatch roof of the O'Connor cottage. In a few minutes, it is ablaze, being fanned by a strong southwesterly breeze. In a short time, before our eyes, the cottage roof is gone. Then the cruel men take battering rams and knock the stone walls of the cottage down. The agent, constable, and soldiers ride on to the next house to tumble. I fear they are going to our own.

Kate and I climb out of the hay shed and run towards home. We can hear Mrs. O'Connor and Mam crying loudly behind us. I know we have to get Meg out of the house before they get there, for Meg will stubbornly allow herself to be burned up in the cottage rather than be pushed around by anyone but Mam and Da.

While we are running home, we find that Meg is already walking to the O'Connor cottage. We tell her what has happened and the three of us go back to be with Mam and Mrs. O'Connor. Mam and Da tell us that the agent, the constable, and the redcoats are going to another neighbor's house but won't be going to our own, for we have paid half our rent. We stay until dusk sitting with the O'Connors in their terrible grief. I can't stop the fear from invading my mind as I imagine our own cottage being tumbled. Da says it can't happen because we've paid half our rent. I don't bother reminding him that the O'Connors had also paid half of their rent. It didn't matter that they had paid it, for there is no justice from the English towards the Irish.

Chapter Eight

TICKETS TO AMERICA

I walk down the narrow rocky road with my Da. He is wearing strips of cloth tied over his boots whose soles have almost completely fallen off. I know his steps are probably painful, but I also know he is confident about our future. We are on our way to purchase tickets for passage to America. America! I love to say the name aloud. Da's resolution to leave Ireland is fierce altogether, and I know it drives away the terrible demons of sadness and hunger. Ever since the tumbling of the O'Connor cottage, I have become more fearful than I have ever been in my life. Our friends, the O'Connors, are living in a little one-roomed structure made out of stone, timber, and clay on the side of the road. All of the neighbors helped them erect it the day after the tumbling of their cottage. I will never forget the horror of the day and now I only feel safe when I'm in the dresser or with my Da. He doesn't know how to drive away my fears, and this is worrisome to me, for he has always sung me a song or told me a story when I have been afraid. I think that is why he has allowed me to come with him on this journey to Queenstown to buy our tickets. It almost feels like a holiday, being alone with Da on the road journeying to a big city. I am wearing some old, laced-up boots of Mam's, but I had to wrap my feet in rags to make them fit properly.

"Are you taking yourself to the Works again, Eoin McCabe?" Sean Flannery asks as he pulls up alongside us in his horse and cart.

"No, Sean, I'm . . . ," Da begins to say.

"No matter where you're going this fine mornin', Eoin, get in, and I'll take you," Sean says, and nods to me as well.

Mam says Sean Flannery is a fortunate one, for he has more land than most farmers. He has land to grow some extra crops besides his potatoes, but he sells them to his own people at prices they can hardly afford. He is despised, though, he, too, pays a very high rent to the landlord.

I know Da doesn't want to ride with Sean and accept any kindness from this evil man. I nudge him to try and say that we shouldn't trust his offer, but Da says he's much obliged for the ride and so we get into the cart and have to sit next to Sean.

"You have the look of someone planning a journey, Eoin McCabe! Are you desertin' your country like so many are doing now?"

"I'm left with the stench of rotting potatoes, Sean, and I have no means to live. It's only a matter of time before our cottage will be torn down like so many who can't pay their rent. My sister, Annie, is across the sea in America and she has welcomed us to live with her."

"The fare will be a pretty penny for the lot of you!" Sean responds. "I doubt if the landlord, the big fella himself, will pay it as some others are doing to rid the land of the non-paying tenants!"

I notice that Da cringes at Sean's words. I stare at Sean's robust and healthy body. I know Mam scolds me when I stare at people, but it's a way of sizing them up and seeing what they're worth. I'd say Sean Flannery is worth nothing and everything at the same time. Da told Mam about the bit of gossip concerning Sean Flannery he heard on his way home from the Works.

Apparently, he is being bribed by the agent to keep quiet about the grain that is being shipped to England while we're all going to the graves with the hunger.

"I've enough fare, Sean. 'Tis for our living that we must leave this land of the dying," Da states firmly. I am proud of his confidence.

"I hear tell that the ships are full of the dying before they arrive in port in America. You'd best be going to the Poorhouse, Eoin McCabe!"

"And the Poorhouse will tear us away from each other. I'll have no talk of it, Sean! I see this land full of luckless men dying before they even reach the port! Hold your tongue! We'll all not perish!" And with that response, my Da put an end to the drudgery of Sean's inquiring and bad news. We passed the rest of our travel in silence.

Arriving in Queenstown, County Cork, a few hours later, Da thanks Sean for the ride and we jump off his cart. Sean calls after him, "I'd be pleased to give you a return ride home. I'll be leaving in a few hours from McGregor's, mind you. It'll be morning by the time we get home, but your feet won't be worn out." He looks at me and smiles. I look away. I don't mind walking home with Da. I didn't want Da accepting a ride with this man who gets fat on evildoings, but to my surprise, Da nods to Sean which means he's grateful for a return ride. When we turn to leave, Sean calls after us again. "And if you're not too proud, I'd also be glad to take you and your family back here to catch the steamer in a few days' time."

I can tell that Da is confused by Sean's kindness. I'm only confused by Da's acceptance of Sean's help, for I see into his wicked heart! Isn't it Sean Flannery, himself, an enemy aligned with the English landlords who do not care that the Irish people are dying? How could we accept his kindness when we have heard these things about the man?

"I'd be grateful for the help out of this country, Sean," Da says, and I feel the rush of red hot anger come to my face. The man smiles and nods at me, but I turn away. Da doesn't notice my bad manners and I'm pleased at my behavior.

Sean drives away, and Da and I look down the street to see a long line of ragged and frail looking people standing in a line for food. Da whispers to me that it's a mission run by the Quakers, a Protestant religious group, who don't care that the Irish are Catholic and not Protestant like themselves. He says they open their soup kitchens to anyone who is suffering from the hunger. I look at Da for a sign from him that we'll be standing in that line for some food, but he shakes his head at me, knowing what I want. I can almost smell the soup cooking, and without thinking, I begin to walk towards the line of people.

"No, Nora, we'll not be going there now. We won't have time," Da says, and moves me in the opposite direction.

We begin walking towards the ticket agent's office. I feel uncomfortable in this city. So many eyes of the hungry people stare at us as we walk by. We see some of our neighbors pass by us covered with filth, their eyes filled with uncertainty, and too weak to greet us as they might have done a few months ago. Da hangs his head in sorrow and shame as we walk by them. Was he thinking what I was thinking? That they will die and we will live in a fine house with a bounty of food in America? When we reach the land agent's office, we stand in line to wait our turn at the window.

"Da, can we help the O'Connors and some of our neighbors when we are in America?" I ask.

"On my oath, we'll do that, Nora. You've a kind heart as your mother," Da answers me. I think I must also have a kind heart as my Da.

"Will we take a ship home again, Da, when the hunger is gone?" I ask.

Da's eyes fill with tears and he turns away from me. I know not to ask him again. He has given me his answer already.

Before we realize it, we are at the ticket window. "Eoin McCabe, how can I be of help to you on this beautiful morn?" the ticket agent asks Da.

"I'm here for the purchase of tickets to America, sir," Da says. The eyebrows of this man, who was another one of the landlord's employees, rose to the top of his forehead.

"To purchase, you say?" he asks, with his eyebrows still stuck to the very top of his head. I chuckle to myself to see such a comical expression.

"To purchase, sir," Da replies. I know Da doesn't want to explain that he has worked on the Relief Works with a dead man's name and sold his livestock so he can now buy his family's passage out of Ireland. Da explained to us last evening that we have to get out before the rest of the rent becomes due. If we pay the rent, he said, there will be no money to buy seed potatoes and livestock. The landlord has given the agent instructions to increase the rent and evict the tenants who can't pay it. The evicted tenants will go to the Poorhouse and he will have to pay a fee for their stay there. This is why the rent has been increased, but the poor Irish tenants have no means to pay it! There has been talk that he and other landlords are going to send the tenants to America as an alternative to supporting them in the Poorhouse.

The ticket agent is incredulous, "Don't you know, McCabe, that Lord Belhord is sending people to America who cannot pay their rent? You fool, McCabe! You must know that the law says there will only be free passage given to those without the means to pay!"

"I want tickets to America, sir," Da says, trying to keep his anger from spilling over.

"If you have money for tickets, McCabe, then you have money for the rent. If you were a wise man, you would have hidden your money and saved it for starting up in America! You would have been able to go to America on Lord Belhord's generosity!" The agent laughs so hard his hat falls off. I feel embarrassed for Da. Maybe this man is right and Da has made a foolish mistake! Da's face is very red, but he answers the ticket agent with surety.

"If I buy tickets to America and give you all the money I possess, Lord Belhord does not have to give me free tickets. He, as usual, will have gained. If I pay my rent, my family will be destitute and it will be his responsibility to send me to America so he doesn't have to feed us in the Poorhouse. If I hid from him that I have money saved, as you suggest I should have done if I were a wise man, it would make me a dishonest and destitute man, and that I will not be! I will pay my own way to America!"

I am so proud of my father, but I can tell the agent is impatient with him.

"How many tickets, McCabe?" he asks.

"Five, sir, I need five." Da lays out his money upon the counter.

After counting the money, the agent's eyebrows went in the opposite direction—down! "You have only enough money for the purchase of three tickets, McCabe! Will you pay your rent instead and remain here and eventually go to the Poorhouse? Surely you don't expect Lord Belhord to give you two free tickets now, do you?"

"No, I cannot stay in Ireland. My mind is made up. What can be done? Can you trust me for the money after I've worked awhile in the new country? Will I give you a promissory note?" Da asks feverishly. I notice his face has now turned pale, for he must feel the weight of hopelessness that I am beginning to feel as well.

"Be gone with you, McCabe! Go sell some other property you've hidden from us and come back and purchase your tickets!"

"I have no other property!" Da shouts, pulling me away as the rain begins to pelt us as if in agreement with our growing despair. We begin walking down the street and then Da stops walking and tells me to stay where I am and not move. He walks back to the ticket agent's window and pushes ahead of the next man standing in line. I can hear people yelling at him. I don't obey Da, but walk closer so I can watch and hear everything that is being said.

"Go back to the end of the line, McCabe!" someone shouts.

"I have something! I have something! Will you take it in exchange for a ticket?" Da asks the ticket agent.

The agent is impatient with Da. His eyebrows, I notice, are in a straight line.

"Get on with it, McCabe!" he commands.

"My dresser! It's an Irish dresser, sir! It possesses a beautiful design, and has been kept from nicks and warping. It's our family's most treasured possession, given to us as a wedding gift from my wife's mother in Dublin."

I can't believe what I'm hearing! Not my dresser! Da is not going to give away my dresser to this wicked agent!

"No, Da!" I cry out as I run and stand by his side. Da looks down at me. I know he's angry at me for interrupting him, and I cling to him.

"Nora, don't say another word or you'll be punished!" I hold my tongue, but I can't control my tears. They pour out of my eyes and down my dress until the front of me is all wet. I'm learning I can cry without sound, but I can't stop the tears from flowing.

The agent is furious with Da, "A dresser! You want to purchase a ticket with a dresser? Do you know how many dressers his Lordship probably already owns, McCabe? What would he want with another!"

"It's expensive . . . "

The agent's eyebrows again shot up to the top of his head.

"It's expensive, is it? Is it New York you're fleeing to, McCabe?"

The agent thinks hard and rubs his bristly chin, pulling down his bottom lip, revealing rotten teeth. I wonder how such an important person as himself could have such a set of teeth as that.

"It's New York, sir," Da replies.

"I have a sister in New York, McCabe. She'll be pining for an English or Irish dresser, whatever it is you call them, but I do believe they originated in England, not Ireland, McCabe. I must be able to trust your word that it's an expensive one and I'll find out for sure when she writes to me of the quality of this dresser. If it's not as you say, you'll wish you had died here in your own country." I can't see anything for the amount of tears coming from my eyes. I can't believe Da is giving away the dresser!

Da stands straight and proud, "Then I'll take it to her, sir!"

The agent laughs but then becomes serious, "Alright then, but what about the fifth ticket you need? The fourth ticket is for the dresser. You still need one more!"

I faint after Da answers the agent. "My sister here in Ireland will watch over my youngest until we send the money for her passage to America," he states confidently.

Chapter Nine

THE PLAN

The blazing fire in the hearth radiates warmth throughout our cottage. An aura of safety and love permeates the room. Anyone looking in our window would not believe we are in the midst of terrible suffering that not only afflicts us, but all of our countrymen.

I sit in the dresser while Mam and my sisters work all day washing their clothing, hair, and packing up the few pieces of china to give to the O'Connors. Mrs. O'Connor will come for our butter churn, pots, and the china after we leave for America. I've been too weak to do anything since my fainting spell in Queenstown. When we were walking away from the ticket agent, Da explained he would never leave me here in Ireland. However, I'm beginning to doubt everyone and everything, even Da. What will we do for the extra ticket? Da didn't explain anything to me, but told me everything would work out for the best. When we got home from purchasing the tickets, I climbed into the dresser and it has been here I have stayed.

"Oh, Nora, such a dramatic one, you are," Meg says as Kate tries to convince me to come out.

"Nora, did you hear what Da said? He said he doesn't want us taking any belongings with us. He said we'll have tortoise-shelled combs and brushes for our hair, beds with soft mattresses to sleep on, and there'll be many dressers in America," Kate says to try and cheer me up.

"But not this dresser, an Irish dresser like our own," I say, thinking about it being given to the ticket agent's sister who probably had one already.

"Come out, Nora, and give yourself a washing," Mam says.

"I'm not going to America!" I scream. After that, no one says anything to me for the rest of the day. Before the hunger came, I never would have gotten away with defying Mam the way I did, but nothing is the same now. Eventually, I come out of the dresser to eat and wash myself, but I'm eager to get back in when it's time for everyone to go to sleep. My head is full of mixed-up feelings about Ireland and America.

I listen to the familiar fire crackle in the hearth. Mam sits mending a dress, waiting for Da to come home. He is out visiting the O'Connors and meeting with some of the men from the neighborhood. When he walks in, I'm beginning to drift off to sleep. I awake with a start when I hear his voice.

"Half the village is dying of the fever, Marion. I've been passing the dying and the dead all day. Men on horseback with cloths over their faces pulling the dead on wagons to empty them into one big grave," he says sadly.

I peek out of the dresser and see Mam go to Da, "Mother Mary and her Son, Jesus, have mercy on the dead!" she cries. "Eoin, now away outside with you and wash the grime off your face."

I notice how tired and hungry Da looks.

"Get me a sup of water, Marion, and are there any of your cakes to eat?"

"Aye, there be two cooking between the leaves of a cabbage Maeve O'Connor gave us."

As Da turns to go outside to clean up, in walks a woman with mangled hair and grime so thick upon her face she is unrecognizable.

"If you please, can ya spare a poor woman a crust of bread?" she pleads.

Mam is aghast by this intrusion and protective of the last bit of food she has managed to save. She screams at the woman to get out of her home.

Da looks surprised by Mam's behavior. As the woman turns to leave their cottage, he says to Mam, "By God, Marion, you'll be at St. Peter's door yourself yet, and you would not want to be turned away!"

The woman walks out of our cottage, unwilling to beg any further. Da goes to the hearth and grabs the cakes that are supposed to be his own to eat. He runs after the woman who has gotten to the road and gives her the food. I have come out of the dresser and watch out the door at the whole scene. I can see by the light of the moon that the woman's cheeks are sunken and her lips are narrow and tight. She looks into Da's face and says, "Get yourself back to your woman." Then she hands him back one of the oaten cakes and says, "Go eat, for I know it must be your evenin' meal. God be praised for your compassion!" She turns away from Da and walks feebly down the road.

Mam is weeping by the fire and I am trying to comfort her when Da comes back in.

"Oh, Eoin, how unlike me to turn a poor woman away from food. This hunger is turning me into something I don't like—yelling at my children, having no hope, and ready to kill the person who takes the food from the mouths of my family!"

Da gathers us into his arms and holds us closely.

"In the dresser," I say to Mam and Da, "I feel hope, I really do. It is the only place I feel it, and I can't ever have it gone from me," I say with all earnestness.

"And so it will be in the dresser you will travel, Nora," Da answers, "for it will be your hiding place when we board the ship to take us to America. You know, I've only three tickets to get us on the ship . . . "

"And the dresser in exchange for a ticket to be given to a woman in New York, but I won't let her have it, Da!" I say.

"You'll not worry, Nora, for it will be a long time from now. What we need to be concerned with is what to do about another ticket. That is why you, Nora, will be hidden as a treasure in the dresser when we board the ship for America."

Mam begins to protest but then she changes her mind and becomes silent. I think she knows it is our only hope and we must be strong. She tucks me into the dresser and kisses me goodnight. I can't remember the last time she has kissed me. My feelings are flying all over my head and heart. I keep trying to get them to calm down but they keep coming like a rainstorm flooding my mind. My dresser will be given to someone else in America. How can it be! But then I begin to think that at least the dresser will be in America, the same country as I will be in, and perhaps I can see it once in awhile. I think about leaving Ireland—the O'Connors, the hills, our cottage—and my heart feels as if it has been broken in half.

Fear is my nighttime visitor. I'm afraid of being on the ship, making a noise in the dresser, and being found out. Then I will be left without my family in Ireland. I'm afraid of drowning in the sea inside the dresser! I'm afraid of . . . I'm afraid of . . . I'm afraid of my very heart that beats so desperately inside of me! As I curl up in the dresser, peace finally comes, tiptoeing into my busy mind and consoling me to sleep.

Chapter Ten

Courage to Leave

"Help, Mam! Help! I can't open my eyes. The fairies have sewn them shut!" I sit up in the dresser and touch my eyes. They're swollen and caked with a hard crust. It is not yet dawn and still very dark outside. Everyone stirs from sleep and hurries to see what is wrong with my eyes. Da lights a candle and Mam looks at my eyes.

"Put a sod of turf on the embers, Meg, and heat some water," she commands.

"Lie back down, child, for there's been no fairy visitin' you in the night. It is just your constant crying that has blown up your eyes and made them crusty. Warm water will loosen them and you'll be seeing again in no time," Mam says.

After my puffy eyes are opened and I can see again, Meg and Kate turn to Da to ask him about our trip to America. They had been sleeping the night before when Da told me about hiding in the dresser on the boat to America.

"What are we going to do for another ticket, Da?" Meg asks.

Da is silent and stands up and walks to the dresser, now empty of its few pieces of china. He strokes its smooth texture with his rough and callused hands.

81

"Look at it, my girls. Is it not bright with hope and as strong as the Irish?" Father's face glows with a peaceful certainty I haven't seen in a long time.

"Listen to me, Meg and Kate," Da says. "I have in my possession three tickets and one Irish dresser that will serve as another ticket. We have four tickets for our passage to Ireland . . . "

"Yes, Da, we know, but there are five of us!" Meg says.

"Aye," and pulling me close to his side, he explains, "and Nora here will be hidden in this dresser with God as her companion . . . "

"Blessed Mother, I don't understand!" Meg exclaims. As usual, she tries to sound like Mam.

"There is little to understand, Meg. Our Nora will hide in the dresser while we cross the sea to America!" Mam explains, tears welling up in her eyes.

Kate comes to my side and hugs me, "Why not let me hide inside of the dresser instead of Nora, Da?"

"No, Kate, I believe our Nora who spends so much time in the dresser already should be the one to hide in it," Da says with confidence.

The day that Sean Flannery arrives to take us to Queenstown in his carriage as he promised, everyone is waiting outside but me. I sit on the floor next to the dresser watching a sunbeam come through the window that creates a dance of memories. I listen to the conversation outside the cottage door.

"I will not demand one coin from you for the journey, McCabe, only some drinking water and good conversation," Sean says with a gleam in his eye, remembering Da's discomfort in talking on the trip to Queenstown.

"The agent told me I need a sea store of food for the journey, Sean," Da says.

"No, McCabe, you don't need anything but your clothes, for I have seen them hauling sacks of oatmeal and biscuits on board. Your fare includes food for the journey, I am almost certain of it," Sean answers.

"Look here," Mam says, "I've made up some bread with the cornmeal you brought me from the Works, Eoin. It's bitter tasting but it'll keep us alive."

I look out the door to see Sean walk over to his wagon and remove a large bundle he has hidden underneath his seat. He hands it to Da and Mam. "It isn't much, but it should last a good two weeks on your journey," he says.

Mam opens it to find dried herring, biscuits, and a sack of oat flour. She drops the parcel and clings to Da to hide her tears. Sean uncomfortably turns away from the embracing couple and works on the wagon to make it ready for the trip. Da picks up the bundle of food and places it next to Kate and Meg who are already on the cart and eager to depart.

My tears begin flowing again because of the kindness of Sean Flannery, but more so because I am leaving behind all I have ever known.

I look around at the empty potato loft above our sleeping corner and at the empty kettle hanging over the dying embers. I look at the worn-out stool that stands crooked next to the hearth and I can imagine Mam sitting on it waiting for Da to return from working in the fields. I can almost hear the squeal of Mr. James Pig and the short-clipped notes of Miss Maggie Hen as I remember them. I can picture Da sitting on a log next to us playing his fiddle over and over. As I look at the dresser that stands near the door ready to be hoisted upon the wagon, a fierce-looking jackdaw crow flies through the window and sits upon the top of it. I scream and run out of the cottage as fast as I can. Everyone in Ireland knows that a crow is an evil omen and a sign of bad luck!

I run into the field of rotten potatoes. The stench is still strong and I almost vomit from it as well as from my fear. I don't know where I'll go but now I know that I can't go to America according to Da's plan. I can't, not after seeing the crow atop the dresser! I fall to the ground in a heap and cling to the coin Da gave me when he told me I'd be hiding in the dresser.

"I won't hide myself in the dresser! I won't! I won't!" I cry. I have such a longing in my heart to have life the way it used to be. I want to see Mam's few pieces of china be put back in the dresser, Da's pipe sitting atop it, and holy water in the tin can to keep the evil away. As I lie crying, I listen to the beautiful singing of a red-winged blackbird over me. It sounds so clear and heartening, I begin to forget my suffering and listen to its song. Then I hear someone moving behind me and look up to see that Mam has followed me to where I am lying. She, too, has heard the melody of the blackbird, for she looks in its direction.

"Mam, an evil crow came into the cottage and sat on the dresser. I cannot go to America now!" I tell her.

"No, pet, it's not the evil omen of the crow that you should be thinking of. It is the good blessing of the blackbird to come singing to you of hope and a new life for all of us. It is not happenstance, daughter. For light is greater than darkness, and the light came after the darkness had tried to bring despair," Mam says.

I know in my heart that what Mam is saying is true. We walk back to the cottage and though I am trembling, I'm beginning to surrender to the notes of the blackbird that has followed us and given me courage.

Chapter Eleven

QUEENSTOWN, CORK

Our trip to Queenstown is quiet and mournful. As early morning surrenders to day, the air becomes wet and muggy. We are sweltering in our layered clothing we have worn to ward off the morning cold and also to carry our few possessions in. The road we're traveling on is rocky and long, and we are continually meeting people who appear before us like skeletons. They are walking to work on the roads for the Relief Works. I don't know how they will have the strength to work, for they can barely walk. I see death devouring humanity for the first time in my life. When we stop to give Sean's horse some rest, we meet a man dragging seaweed from the ocean to lay upon his potato field.

Da speaks to the man, "Why do you use your last body's heat, my man, when your crop is dead, as is all our crops of potatoes all over Ireland!"

The old man, stooped over and filthy, answers, "This fertilizer, this hair of the mermaids, is a gift from the sea." He clutches the seaweed, his eyes bloodshot and hardly open. "I will gather the life from the sea and lay it upon my crop, hoping and praying God Almighty will raise it up as He did Lazarus."

I shiver even though I'm too warm in my clothing, and clutch the small, delicate, blue and white teapot Mam has given me to hide. I have never seen

death like this. Only in the pigs when they are slaughtered. Now my eyes behold people lying in ditches
looking like they, too, have been struck down and
are ready to be sold like the pigs in the market. I
wonder if God sees them all alike—the animals and
the people together! I know I'm becoming an old child
and feel more than gnawing hunger in my belly. I
have a longing in my soul that I cannot explain.

It is very late in the day when the wagon reaches
Queenstown and we climb down. Da argues with Sean
about giving him some coins to pay for his journey
but Sean will not take anything. I accidentally catch
my shawl on a nail as I'm letting myself down from
Sean's wagon. As I free myself from the nail, the lid it
was attached to comes open and I stare in disbelief.
Inside the box, I see enough grain to feed all of our
neighbors!

"You are wicked, Sean Flannery!" I scream at him.
"You'd rather help the English than take care of your
own people!"

Mam pulls me to herself, "Quiet, child, 'tis not
your concern."

Sean drops his head onto his chest and takes the
strong words I beat him with.

"She speaks the truth. Leave her be. She's a special child and she'll be your guiding light in many
ways," Sean says of me.

I hide my face in my mother's skirts as my heart
pounds within me. It is a grave wrongdoing to speak
with disrespect to any adult, especially one outside
the family.

No one knows what to do or say. Kate and Meg
sit playing with their hair, their eyes cast down. I continue to cling to Mam's skirts and Da is fidgeting with
the dresser that has been strapped with a rope to prevent the drawers from falling out. The lower part of
the dresser has been left unstrapped, for it is there
that I will hide myself.

Standing by the General Store is a fiddler beginning his round of reels and jigs that will bring him a few coins. It's hard for me to imagine anyone having the strength to celebrate life with music and dancing. The old fiddler is playing a reel and a few of the children standing around him begin to dance. Without thinking, I break away from Mam and go to dance with them. I almost fall to the ground at first, for I'm weak from eating poorly over the last few months. People begin milling around us and someone points at me and says, "Faith, but that one mixes her legs well!" I am beaming with joy I haven't felt in a long time and I feel energy coming into my frail body while I lift my legs and dance on my toes.

When I return to the carriage, Sean walks to where Da is working on the dresser.

"Will you help me, Eoin? Will you help me with this large crate of grain?" he asks.

I can tell Da is confused and he doesn't answer him.

"I need to carry it to the Quakers for their soup line, and it is right heavy to do it alone," Sean says.

I go with Da and Sean to give the grain to the Quakers. I know Sean must have known I'm curious to see if he will give the grain to feed the hungry. After leaving it with the Quakers, Sean says, "I've a cousin living on Fair Lane who'd be willing to put your family up for the night as the *Star* sails tomorrow in the morn. Tea and bread filled with sweets for you especially, Nora," he says, turning to me and smiling.

We spend our last evening in Ireland in Sean's cousin's cottage. It is full of warmth and hospitality but I sleep restlessly waiting for the morning to come.

The next day, we all try to drink in each familiar sight while we stand waiting in line to sail across the sea. The rising sun casts its rays across us like a mother's arms of warmth. The sun has not shone for days, but it is now shining on us before our exodus.

"Look, everyone, the sun is bidding us farewell!" No one seems to hear me, for there are sobbing embraces of relatives and people coming out of the soup lines to say goodbye. Many who are remaining in Ireland long to leave as well, but most pity us travelers for having to take leave because we cannot thrive in our native land. Each of us presses a foot into the ground, trying to leave a lasting footprint. I reach down and pick up some soil, this soil that will not grow potatoes for us, and place it in the little teapot in my bundle.

As we stand in line to board, I see the biggest ship I've ever seen in my life, the *Star*.

"That is the ship, Nora, that will become our salvation," Da whispers in my ear. I begin to feel the familiar fear again. It begins in the bottom of my belly and works its way up into my mind where it feels like it will become a fever. I take deep breaths to keep myself from running away. The dresser stands next to me and there is great pandemonium going on at the front of the line. I hear screams of protest from family members who are saying goodbye to their loved ones leaving Ireland, and the crew of the ship trying to quiet the crowd. I'm tired and hungry, for the morning has turned to day and I'm only able to nibble on some oat cakes and dried herring. I watch some of the passengers as their few belongings are oftentimes flung on board. Some are being pulled on by crew members for they're frightened to get on the boat.

"How will I stay in the dresser in one piece?" I think while the fear I've tried to keep quiet begins to creep into my mind again. Then my thoughts are suddenly interrupted by a familiar voice beside me.

"Eoin McCabe, my uncle, Eoin McCabe! I've been searching all over Ireland for you!" cries a young man about sixteen years old. It's Michael, a cousin, who lives in County Kerry. I know Da sent word to our relatives about our departure to America. I remember thinking he was going to send me to them until he had enough money to purchase me a ticket to America.

I noticed how changed Michael is. His youth has been stolen from him and he looks older than sixteen years.

"It's Cousin Michael!" I cry out and run from the line to Michael, who is a picture of familiarity even though his appearance is so altered.

"Oh, Michael, you've come to board the ship with us!" I say.

Michael sits down on the ground, proclaiming he's exhausted from walking and begging for food. I motion to Mam and Mam pulls a small biscuit from her shawl and gives it to Michael. He eats it all in one bite and says, "We are but starving and out of our home. The soldiers tumbled it a few days ago." He puts his head in his hands because of his shame and tiredness.

I kneel down beside Michael, and then Da covers his face with his large-jointed hands. For the first time in our lives, my sisters and I watch our Da cry.

Michael continues to share his news, "Lord Athlene evicted over a thousand people in our parish. We've taken some of our old roof they tore down and made us a shelter three feet deep. 'Tis nothin' but a hole in the earth, Uncle. We've only cabbage leaves and nettles to eat."

I see Da draw Michael close to him, and while he weeps, he gives him some coins from his pocket. It's only a pittance, certainly not enough for my ticket, but it will help Michael and his family. It was to be the start-up money for when we arrive in America, but I know Da doesn't care about that right now. I know that if we just get ourselves to America, it will be enough.

"Take it, Michael, take it," Da says to Michael. "Buy some food and tell your father and mother I'll be sending more after we're settled in the new country."

Michael is crying as well, and pours out his feelings that must have been building up within him on his journey to Queenstown, "I saw death on the roadside, Uncle. A neighbor and a priest, I did see . . . no one helped, no one stopped to help . . . "

"God and His Son shall preserve the likes of us, Michael. That I know, and if it is not so, there will be a remnant left here to stand in for us!" Da says to Michael.

A soldier patrolling the street walks up to us to tell us that we'll lose our place on board if we do not stay in line.

Michael is clasped dearly to each one of us and then we say goodbye. With a heavy heart for Michael and his family, I know I must forget my feelings and prepare myself for the journey in the dresser.

"Shhh, Nora, don't you cry, pet, ye must be brave. It's time. It's time for you to go into the dresser," Da says.

I feel dizzy and my mind begins to swirl like the waves of a stormy sea, making me feel as if I'm already floating on the water.

"What if I cannot breathe?" I think. "And what if everyone forgets me?" Then I faint for the second time in my life.

Chapter Twelve

INSIDE THE DRESSER

I wake up in Da's arms as he struggles to hold me so no one will see. If any of us become ill, we won't be allowed to get on the ship. Mam takes the end of her shawl and wets it in some of our drinking water. She washes my face until I feel fully awake. When I open my eyes, I realize that nothing has changed. Feeling frightened has not changed anything at all. I am still going to have to get into the dresser alone and go across the sea to America. I am going to have to trust my Da and trust God, and if I die, I will wake up in heaven. Do I really believe this? I don't know if I do, but I have to pretend that I do right now so I can get in the dresser.

"I think I'm ready, Da," I say. Mam takes her shawl from around her waist as well as my own, and places them inside the dresser, trying to make it comfortable for me. My family surrounds the dresser so no one will see what is about to take place. I look into each face of my family, and give each one a hug. I cling to Kate longer than anyone else. My lovely Kate who helps me feel brave because she is really the brave one. Then I climb into the dresser. Mam takes some bread and herring and hands them to me.

"Save it, pet. Don't utter a word, not even your prayers aloud. We'll stay alongside the dresser as much as possible, and if we get separated, we won't be that far away."

My hair is matted to my head because I'm over-heated, and as soon as I enter the dresser, I feel tired as well as the familiar feeling of being at home inside the dresser. I nestle into the shawls and place the bread and herring beside me. Then I close my eyes to try and sleep, remembering fainting and how good it felt to be far away from my fear and dread.

"*A storin,*" Da whispers to me, "I have never loved you as much as I do now. Remember not to worry when the dresser is moved. You'll be tossed about when it's being taken upon the ship, but the doors will be held together by the straps. Don't cry out! When we're settled in a berth, we'll take you out when no one is looking."

Da and Sean had cut a small hole in the side of the sturdy dresser before they left the cottage. It's the only way for me to get some air while I'm inside. And so I try to sleep cradled in the dresser that has be-come my refuge a long time before this day has come. Maybe it had prepared me for this time when I must cross the sea.

I think about the death I have seen on the way to port. I know even though death is strong, life never stops going on, like the reappearing sun that has been hidden behind the clouds for days. I think about the clinging family members that have to be pulled apart. There was a distraught woman who pulled a baby out of her sister's arms and ran down the street scream-ing that not all of her family was going to leave Ire-land. There was fighting when some farmers watched grain and livestock being put on another ship bound for England. They tried to prevent it from leaving the port by lashing out with sticks and rocks. The soldiers beat them back, "You are a rebellious and ungrateful lot. Go home and work your fields!"

I'm very drowsy but I can feel the dresser being hoisted onto the deck, a crew member grunting and complaining that there is not enough room for people let alone furniture.

"Hurry along, hurry along!" shouts the crew. I hear Meg complaining and Kate trying to soften her anger as they walk up the plank behind the dresser. When everyone is on board, I hear a loud voice shouting. "Halt, you! And you! All of you! Leave your belongings and go back down to pass before the ship doctor! You can't board without being checked by the doctor! If you don't pass his inspection, you don't board! We'll have to throw your things off the ship!"

I know I can't take the chance of having anyone see me in the dresser, but I need to find out what is going to happen to my family. I push on the door of the cupboard so the strap stretches to where I can peer out. The dresser is at the top of the entrance to the ship and the front of it is facing down the plank so I can see everything that is taking place. I see that Mam is ignoring the crewman and trying to squeeze past some others. Then I see a couple of people spill over into the water as they try to get on board, but they quickly get to shore and stand dripping wet before the doctor. Then a sailor appears at Mam's side and tries to escort her back down the plank. "No, Mam, don't leave me!" I want to shout but I keep still. The rest of my family has obeyed and are already standing before the doctor. He sits in a booth and merely glances at each passenger's throat as they walk by. Then a crewman takes their tickets. If a crippled person stands before him, the doctor shouts, "No board!"

Mam pulls away from the sailor, "No! No! My baby is already on board!" The sailor lets her go and tells her to get the baby and go back down the plank to be seen by the doctor. Mam knows she can't retrieve me and go back down the plank to see the doctor. It would then be known there is no ticket for me. I can tell she is frantic and doesn't want to leave me in the dresser alone. I don't want her to leave me either! Oh, how I want to crawl out and touch her and have her hold my hand!

"Nora," Mam whispers through the cupboard doors of the dresser when she gets away from the sailor.

"I hear you, Mam," I say, still looking out of the cupboard door. I see people milling around the deck wondering where they're going to bunk, people who have already seen the doctor and given their ticket to board the ship. The sailor who let her on board to retrieve me is waiting for her to get the baby that is nowhere to be seen! "Oh, Mam, think fast," I whisper. There's an old woman standing next to her and the dresser. She looks pleadingly at Mam and says, "Please, by the grace of God, do ya have some bread for an old woman?" Mam looks at her protruding stomach. I have learned that this is a sign of starvation. Mam gives her some bread. Another young woman, wearing a disheveled, blue-flowered dress and a cream-colored bonnet, comes near Mam and the dresser. My hand is getting cramped trying to see everything, and I let go of the strap on the cupboard. I lose sight of the young woman and Mam, but I can hear everything that is being said.

"'Tis a lovely dresser! It looks like Lord Boothby's, it does!" the woman says admiringly. "There's no one alive in Limerick, it seems, except my aunt and her brood. Lord Boothby is giving out food, they say. To his tenants and to Father O'Brien, who are all thin as rails. I've got myself a ticket to America and I'll never return to this awful place. Lord Boothby bought my ticket, for he said I needed to go before I got myself into trouble. I've always worked for Lord Boothby and his family while living with my aunt and trying to get myself an education."

The young woman talks incessantly and I hear Mam try to interrupt her but she's unsuccessful.

"My name's Maggie," she continues, "and I'm rightly pleased to meet you and this lovely dresser . . . "

"Maggie, I've got to go and find the rest of my family," Mam says nervously. "Will you stay next to the dresser and watch it with your life?"

"Yes, but . . . ," Maggie answers, and then I hear Mam leave and walk down the plank. Her footsteps echo in my head, as they are a sign of growing despair for me.

I hear Maggie sigh and I feel her touching the dresser.

"What a strong piece of furniture . . . stronger than me, I think . . . ," Maggie says to herself.

"Me, too," I reply, no longer able to keep quiet.

Maggie must be looking all around to see who has spoken to her.

"Me, too," I say again.

I hear Maggie jump to her feet and then sit down again.

"I must be starvin' to death and hearing the voice of an angel!" she says.

I tap on the dresser and whisper loudly, "Where did my Mam go?"

Maggie must be surprised, but before she can say anything, I hear loud voices singing out a roll call for a ship called the *Seabird*. "Paddy Boyle, come here awhile—Joseph Burns come down—*Eoin McCabe* now show your bones."

"Do you know why Da's name is being sung?" I ask. "Do you know why he's being called to board another ship and not the *Star?*"

Maggie moves aside a strap and peeks through the door of the cupboard.

"I want Mam and Da!" I shout, unable to be strong and quiet any longer. "Why are they going on another ship?" I'm feeling as if I'll faint again, but I will myself to be strong.

A few people in the crowd look over at us when they hear me shout. Maggie shuts the cupboard tight and says, "I was only calling for my mammy," and everyone goes back to what they were doing. A sailor comes walking up to Maggie. "Give me your name, lass," he commands.

Maggie kicks her foot against the dresser to try and signal to me to remain quiet. I'm sure she doesn't know why I'm in the dresser, but she probably knows it should be kept a secret.

"My name's Maggie. Maggie O'Houlihan. Maggie O'Houlihan from County . . . County . . . Do you want to know my birth county or Lord Boothby's county where I worked, sir?"

"Never mind! Have you seen the doctor?" he asks. I can't help myself. I have to see what is happening. I carefully push on the cupboard door to peer out again.

"Surely the doctor saw me, sir, and I'm as healthy as a heifer, I am, though a wee bit hungry. Is the ration to be given soon, sir? Lord Boothby said I'd be well fed on this ship . . . ," Maggie answers the sailor.

"Quit the prattling, girl, you'll eat when it's time," the large whiskered sailor wearing red suspenders that hook onto his pants that hang below his huge belly, says to Maggie. I stare in disbelief and can't imagine there is that much food in all of Ireland to make such a fat one as that!

I listen to everything but stay very still. I don't know where my Mam and family have gone, but it will be no good for me to come out of the dresser without a ticket and be thrown off the ship.

"Whose dresser is this?" the sailor asks. He pushes and then pulls at the straps.

"Lord Boothby's, sir, but I am to take it . . . ," Maggie begins, but is interrupted by a fight that has begun between some men trying to claim a bag of oats for themselves. The sailor forgets about the dresser and goes to stop the fight.

After the sailor has left, Maggie removes a strap and peers into the dresser.

"Oh, girl," she says, "you've a stench about you that's terrible!"

"I've had an accident," I say with remorse, for I had hoped no one would notice until Mam was with me to help clean me up.

"Where is my Mam?" I ask Maggie, my tears soaking the front of my dress.

"Your Mam asked me to watch the dresser and I had no idea a child as yourself was in it. Then the sailor asked me all kinds of questions and I'm wondering where I'll be sleeping . . . "

I begin to cry aloud, unable to control my emotions again, "I want my Mam!" I'm so afraid of being separated from my family.

"Shhh, child, I'll take good care of you until she comes back. You need not worry over your soiled clothing, for Lord Boothby's daughter gave me a couple of her old dresses to take with me on my journey. And they're not really old, mind you, just old to her, but to me, they're as new as if I had picked them out of one of those fancy stores . . . "

"Please, miss, what's your name?" I ask between sobs.

"Maggie. Short for Margaret. My name's Margaret. Margaret O'Houlihan. I've been employed as a maid, gardener, cook, and just about ran the great estate of Lord Roland Boothby in County Limerick for as long as I can remember. But then with the potatoes rotting and all, and nothing left for the farmers, Lord Boothby decided to move to England. He put me on this ship, he did. A ship to where in America, I don't know, but he said they'd feed me well . . . " Maggie looks around longingly and continues, "So far I haven't seen any food."

"My name's Nora and I've got a wee bit of biscuit and herring to share with you," I say.

Maggie and I eat hungrily and Maggie talks about everything under the sun and moon. I listen half-heartedly but doze off and on, remembering how good it feels to escape into sleep.

"Nora, girl, don't sleep . . . wait here and I'll find us some water to wash you in and you can change your clothes . . . ," Maggie says.

Another sailor walks over to Maggie and the dresser. "Remove yourself to below the deck at once. There's no room in the cabins. Come now, move quickly."

"No! No!" I cry out.

Maggie jumps in front of the dresser and says quickly, "Oh please sir, don't mind my sister, she's afraid and climbed into the dresser to hide . . . " Maggie turns towards the dresser and speaks to me, "Come along, sister, our father is waiting on the other side of this great blue sea in a port called . . . a port called . . . America!"

"I can't move this dresser and break my back taking it below deck. Have you permission to bring it on board?" the sailor asks.

"Oh yes, of course, we did get permission from Lord Boothby of County Limerick who insisted we take it to his sister in America," Maggie lies.

The sailor is puzzled. He hasn't seen many of the poor people take any furniture on ship with them, just a few chests and some pots and pans.

A young man comes walking by Maggie and the sailor, and says, "A fine looking dresser you have there!"

I peek out of the cupboard and notice this young man doesn't look like any of the poor people of Ireland, not even like the landlord and his household. He is wearing a pressed tweed jacket, neat trousers, and is clean-shaven. He has also taken his hat off as he speaks to Maggie.

"And if it is so fine a dresser, sir, you'll think nothing of it to offer your strength to help me carry it below deck for the young woman and her Lord Boothby!" the sailor says.

The young man smiles, "I'll be honored to do an act of kindness for a lovely young woman."

I watch Maggie blush. I have never seen such a man as handsome in all of Ireland. I climb out of the dresser, hoping the sailor will believe what Maggie said about me being her sister. As I struggle to get out, the teapot Mam had given me crashes to the floor and the soil I have hidden away in it spills. I begin picking up the pieces, cutting myself as I do.

"I won't cry!" I say to myself, trying to hold back my tears. Then I look up at the sailor's beard and it appears to me as if it is hanging below his knees! When I look at the young gentleman's hat that he has put back on his head, it seems to reach way up into the clouds. The last thing I remember before I faint the third time in my life is the wilted shamrock that's hanging out of the young gentleman's pocket. Or is it?

Chapter Thirteen

On Board the *Star*

I awake below deck in the steerage area, which is very hot and smells like Miss Pretty, my magic cow. I have been placed on a wooden bunk and I'm almost certain my dresser is gone. Maggie tells me that the captain or his first mate will be down soon to do a roll call.

"I don't have a ticket, Maggie, and now I don't have my dresser," I say to her. I blink to try and see in the dark narrow dungeonlike hold of the ship.

"The dresser is over in the corner. Help me move it," Maggie says. We push the dresser through the crowd of people and place it next to our bunk.

"Get in the dresser, pet, or you'll be thrown off ship, and I, too, will be thrown off for keeping you with me!" Maggie says.

"Where's my Mam?" I ask, suddenly remembering my plight. My heart beats rapidly and my eyes adjust enough to see that this hold below the deck of the ship is filled with passengers on the bunks. It's very quiet for there being so many people in such a small cramped area. I can see that there aren't enough bunks for some of the passengers. They are scrambling over one another trying to find a resting place on their bundles and chests they have brought with them.

"Get in, get in!" Maggie whispers loudly, as she pushes me into the dresser. The dresser sits next to two bunks that are lined up against the wall. Maggie has chosen the bottom bunk and a family of four hurry to fit into the top one. There is little ventilation and I feel like I might faint again. Maggie is closing the doors and tying the straps around them. I curl up in the dresser, clutching the shawls, and close my eyes. I imagine I smell my mother's cooking upon the hearth—fadge, a delicious potato bread with pats of butter in pretty designs Meg would make to melt upon the bread.

I try to find the few things I have brought with me—a coin from Da, the pieces of the broken teapot wrapped up in cloth . . . but where is Da's fiddle and bow? My heart sinks as I realize that I have forgotten to hide them! I hope that Da has them with him. He played the sad song about leaving Ireland just before we left and that was the last time I remember seeing his fiddle.

"Oh Da, please keep it with you!" I say aloud in a prayer. As I lie in the dresser, I listen for the sound of him playing his fiddle. If only I could hear Da playing music on this ship, I would know we are all safe.

"Kate, you'd make me feel safe if you were with me," I say to myself sadly. I feel the bandaged cut on my finger and wonder who has taken care of it for me. I think it must have been Maggie. She's a lovely lass but talks ever so much, but I'm grateful she's here with me until my family finds me. I hope that no one noticed me crawling into the dresser. It seems everyone is madly trying to find a place on a bunk or on the floor and they haven't been paying any attention to me. Many of the bunks look like they're already filled with three or four people. I don't know how people will be able to lie down on any of them so cramped together. I'll have to share this bunk with my family, too.

"You'd be crazy to not share your bunk with us, miss," I hear a woman say to Maggie, "for there are four of us atop this one and only but one of you down there."

Maggie told me she didn't want to share her bunk with anyone and had sprawled across the length of it. Besides, we both knew I would want to come out and sit with her from time to time on the bunk. And what if my family showed up and needed a place to sleep?

"I'm saving it for someone," I hear Maggie say.

"If you're still saving it by the time the ship sets sail, it'll have to be shared by us," responded the woman defiantly.

I close my eyes to sleep, and as I try to stretch, I feel something hard in the corner of the cupboard. It's a package and when I open it, I can't believe my eyes.

"Maggie, open up, open up!" I shout, "'Tis the work of the fairies!"

Maggie opens the cupboard and I tumble out clutching the large package that contains a few pounds of herring and biscuits.

"There's enough food for all of us down here in this stinking hold!" I say loudly.

"Shhh!" Maggie whispers, as she takes the package from me and hides it back inside the dresser.

Just then a loud and deafening blast comes from above the steerage. I scramble into a corner of the bunk and cower in fear. Cries of alarm sweep across the room.

"Why are they firing the blunderbuss?" people ask one another.

"Make a path for the captain, make a path!" a sailor yells as he comes down the stairs to the hold and begins kicking at people and their belongings.

I quickly get inside the dresser again and Maggie ties the straps into place. I peek through the door and see a tattered young man walk over to Maggie.

"I see the stash of food you're hoarding, miss! There's enough of us Irish who've been cheated out of our rations on this ship. We don't need you to be keeping what is rightly ours."

"I don't have to give you anything!" Maggie replies, her arms folded in front of her.

"If you don't give me some of the food you're keeping, miss, I'll tell the captain. I'll shout it out that you have your sister and some food in that dresser there!" he threatens.

I notice that this man's face is hollow and merely a skull with a little bit of skin hanging onto it.

"Give him some food, Maggie," I say through the doors of the cupboard. Maggie reluctantly opens the cupboard up and I hand her some of the food for the angry man.

"Here, take this, and be gone from me!" she whispers loudly.

Maggie quickly re-ties the straps on the dresser, climbs onto the bunk, and we wait for the captain to come. I'm fearful that many of the people in the steerage know I'm in the dresser and they'll be telling the captain. I'm holding back my tears as I think about being thrown out of the ship. As the captain calls out the names of the passengers, no one says a word about me in the dresser.

I listen for the names of my family to be called out by the captain for roll call, but he leaves the hold without mentioning them.

"They must have gotten better sleeping quarters somewhere else, for this ship is very large," I say to Maggie. I'm confident I'll be able to find them later and share the food I found in the dresser. There is no air in the hold and it is stifling hot and very damp. I soon fall into a deep sleep, dreaming of the dresser sliding back down the plank and landing at the feet of my family.

Chapter Fourteen

SAILING AWAY FROM HOME

The *Star* is sailing down the River Lee away from Queenstown, County Cork, towards the great Atlantic. Queenstown is really called Cobh Harbor, its rightful name before the English conquered Ireland. I think of it as a harbor of tears because of all the weeping and wailing I saw there before we boarded the *Star*. I wake hours later and feel the sway of our ship going over strong waves. If I weren't so frightened by this new sensation and in not having my family with me, I might enjoy all the rocking on the sea. I am certain that my family must be up on deck preparing our evening meal.

"Maggie, are you there?" I whisper while tapping lightly on the cupboard.

"I'm here, Nora. Do you want to come out? I'll take you to the deck for some air. There's so many people milling about, they'll never know you as an extra without a ticket."

"Shhh, Maggie, don't even say I don't have a ticket!"

I climb out of the dresser and my body feels stiff. I'm hungry and remember the biscuits and herring I mysteriously found inside the dresser.

"Let's go up on deck and bring the food with us," I say to Maggie. I reach for the food, give some to Maggie, and because we're so hungry, we begin eating. My eyes adjust to the dark hold and I look around me. I see some desperate-looking faces staring at me from their bunks, and my heart aches for them. I can't eat while everyone else is watching me. I quickly stuff a few bites into my mouth and get up from the bunk with the bundle of food. I begin to walk up and down the aisle of the steerage and pass out all the food until it is gone. I climb back onto the bunk to an astonished Maggie.

"Didn't you think, girl, that we might have to eat again on this journey?" Maggie asks angrily.

"The rations will be coming, and besides, my Mam taught me to halve the potato with anyone who needs it, and so I have. It wasn't ours to keep, for it must have been given to us from heaven," I say confidently.

Maggie and I climb up to the deck and find a firebox with people of all ages surrounding it. Some of the passengers who have brought food to be cooked are doing it over the fire. It smells delicious. Rations haven't been given out yet, and there are many hungry people who haven't brought food with them who are standing around hoping for some crumbs. As we approach the crowd, we notice that there is merriment all around in spite of the hunger and pain in the people's faces. I can hardly believe it, for there had been nothing but weeping and moaning just hours before as people said goodbye to Ireland. I suddenly think I hear the sounds of a fiddle and beg Maggie to walk with me around the ship to look for Da.

Maggie and I walk the full length of the ship and I peer into the faces of each person but do not find the familiar faces of my family.

"Have you seen Eoin and Marion McCabe and his daughters?" I ask from time to time.

"Is there anyone here from Kinsale?" I cry out.

The answer is always that no one has seen any McCabes from Kinsale, and I begin to feel myself weaken with fear.

"Oh, Maggie, they have to be somewhere. Will we go up to the deck again and have another look for them?" I ask after we have gone down to our bunks.

"You're not going to believe it, are you, Nora, if they got left behind. I have a good feeling your Mam and the rest of them will be on the next ship to America, so we need to make the best of it all then," Maggie says while I give in to my tears.

Maggie and I go back to the deck and walk all around again. I'm not willing to believe my family is on another ship. There is jesting and singing around the fireboxes while oatmeal cakes cook on the fire. The sails are set to the breeze and the *Star* glides through a sea of liquid fire.

"How lovely is this water that I've never taken notice of before!" I exclaim, as Maggie and I pause in our search to look out at the sea.

"There's evenin' prayers in the hold, one is in Irish and the other in English," the captain's mate announces as he walks the deck.

"I haven't been saying my prayers since Lord Boothby's daughter made fun of me," Maggie says.

"We'll go, then, and you'll take it up again as you should," I say firmly to my new friend. We go back down in the hold to find the evening prayers in Irish.

After Maggie and I have gotten properly blessed, we prepare ourselves for a good night's sleep. Already I'm beginning to feel the life I had in Ireland with Miss Maggie Hen, Mr. James Pig, and being hungry is being left far behind me. Even though I'm filled with worry for my family, this evening I feel something of a light-heartedness I haven't felt in a long time.

As I nestle inside the dresser, I can smell the scent of my mother on her shawl and I'm comforted by this and the gentle rocking of the *Star* as it dares to cross the Atlantic to America.

For the next two weeks, Maggie and I traverse the top and bottom of the ship in search for my family. We never find them and the ache in my heart never wanes but I feel stronger because I'm learning to trust each moment, and no more than each moment, as it comes.

"If there be a God, and I can't help but believe it, nothing can harm me without him knowing it!" I say to Maggie who never wants to do the evening prayers.

Maggie and I haven't seen the kind young gentleman who assisted us with the dresser. We have heard people talking about there being such a person who stays in the captain and his wife's quarters. I wonder if it was him who left the bundle of food for us when we first boarded the ship and needed help moving the dresser into the hold.

A few days into the journey, the captain's mate took charge of the rations which were held in the depot off the hold. He instructed the crew to disburse a pound of meal for each adult, a half pound for children under fourteen, and a third for each child under seven. It is up to everyone to gather around the fireboxes and cook their own food. It is always a challenge to get to the fire because of the crowd. After almost two weeks eating this way, I'm learning how to make sure I get my share of the food.

"Come here, child, and I'll cook your oaten cake right along with me Peggy's," a mother says to me, seeing that I'm a child alone on the *Star*. Maggie eyes me jealously, for she will have to wait her turn, and it sometimes takes two hours to crowd in to get to the fire. The woman who cooks my cake has three wee ones, and people let her in for the sake of her children. The fire is very hot and everyone is in such a hurry that oftentimes the oatmeal griddle cakes are burned on the outside and uncooked on the inside. Twice a week, the mate gives everyone a small piece of salt pork to go along with the meal. I eagerly wait for the salt pork, as it's something I've never had even once a week in Ireland.

Thus far, the journey has been easy except for everyone getting a trifle dizzy from the rocking of the ship and there never being enough water for bathing. Once the mate shouted that another ship could be seen in the east and everyone scrambled to look. I know my family must be on that ship, coming right behind me, and it will be a few more days before we can be together. Every night I clutch the coin Da gave me while I say my evening prayers. For two weeks aboard the *Star*, all goes as well as can be expected, except for me missing my family something fierce.

Chapter Fifteen

A Stranger in the Dark

"Water, for God's sake, give me some water!" cries the mother on the bunk above ours. One of her children has slept with Maggie every night since the ship left Queenstown and my family never boarded the ship. No one ever questions why I sleep in the dresser, for they must understand I'm a child missing my family.

I am overcome with grief for the people who have taken ill with the ship fever. I can hardly sleep at night because of all the groans of agony surrounding me. It is possible that Maggie and I will get sick, too. And I can't help thinking that maybe my family is suffering from the fever aboard another ship.

"Why don't they give that woman more water, Maggie?" I ask one evening as we lie on the bunk listening to the cries for more water.

"The supply of water is scanty, Nora. Don't you remember that three casks were leaking?"

I am only sleeping a few hours every night. One morning I awaken before the sun has risen. There's a biting chill in the dark and damp hold. I can hear the sounds of snoring and moaning throughout the room. Maggie is no longer strapping me into the dresser at night because I don't want to awaken her when I need to relieve myself. I always climb out on my own and go to the corner of the hold behind a curtain to use a small bucket that will be emptied in the morning. It is terribly embarrassing, for I never know when there might be someone else needing to use it at the same time.

This early morning, I climb out of the dresser and wrap myself in Mam's shawl. I'm wearing one of Maggie's dresses and it is much too long, as well as being soiled and wrinkled because I have been wearing it for over a week now without washing it. There's a large tub of water and hand soap atop the deck the crew provides us with from time to time, but it is difficult getting a turn to wash clothing because of the crowd of women using it. I have to keep telling myself that soon I will be in America and meeting my family on a ship that will sail into the New York Harbor next to the *Star*. Aunt Bridget will be waiting, and on our first night there we'll have a soft bed and warm water to bathe in. I will wear dresses made of silk and lace, and Mam will plait my hair and adorn it with red ribbons. Da will play his fiddle and we'll sit around the hearth. I dream of this every day and I can almost taste the food and feel the soft feather bed!

I am full of thoughts about America this morning as I walk down the hold to use the bucket when I bump into something . . . no, not something . . . someone! My heart skips and it feels as if it has missed a few beats. Will I even have a heart in tact when I reach America, for all the new feelings I'm experiencing in it! I reach out in front of me and feel coarse material and inhale a sour smell. It's very dark and no one is allowed to light candles in the hold for fear of fire on the wooden ship. Everyone has to get used to walking in the dark as if they are blind. "Who am I touching in the middle of the night?" I wonder, as my heart beats so hard it is all I can hear.

"Shhh, don't utter a word!" a deep voice whispers, and my arm is tightly grasped.

"Please, I'm only going to use the bucket," I whisper back, feeling even more frightened by the sharp demand of this voice.

"After you use the bucket, I need you to come to the deck. I've been waiting for you to wake up," the voice replies.

"Please then, let me go . . . and I promise to come to the deck," I say, thinking that I will wake Maggie and ask her for help.

As if he can read my thoughts, he says, "Don't go waking up your sister. Come to the deck alone!"

"The passengers aren't allowed on the deck in the night. I heard the mate say he will throw us overboard if he finds us up there after our evening prayers!" I whisper back frantically.

"You'll not be thrown overboard," he says. "If you don't come, I'll find you in your dresser. I also know you don't have a ticket to be on board this ship!"

I shudder and begin to whimper, thinking about this smelly creature waiting for me in the night. I can't tell, but I think that he might be just a boy a few years older than me. I don't know if I have enough courage to follow him as he is demanding me to. And I don't know if it is courage I need. Maybe I should wake up the captain or begin shouting to wake everyone on the ship. Maybe he is a criminal who will kill us all.

"Stop crying. You'll be safe," he says, as if he is reading my thoughts again. I hurry to use the bucket, hoping he doesn't listen or try to watch me.

If I wake Maggie, she might become hysterical and wake the whole ship. If I scream for help, everyone will come running. Either way, I'll be found out and thrown into the sea! I finish using the bucket and take in long deep breaths. I pray quietly and then fumble through the dark, making my way to the deck. Then I hear the voice of the strange young man again as he reaches for me at the top of the deck.

"I'm here! Don't make a noise!" he whispers loudly. The moon is brilliant and lights up the whole deck. I look into the face of a miserable looking creature whose head looks grossly large and misshapen. His skin is sallow and his eyes are glassy. He is only a boy about Meg's age! When he moves his head towards me, I realize it had been a shadow from the moon that made his head look so out of shape. However, he still looks like an odd sight to me. At least he's not a monster! I think.

"What do you want from me?" I ask, trembling from the cold and my fear. Just then we hear the voices of some sailors on the deck.

"She's goin' full sail southward at seven knots an hour. We're gaining very little longitude," one says to the other.

"Crouch down!" the boy whispers as he pulls me to the floor of the deck. We stay there quietly until the sailors disappear into a cabin.

I stand and straighten out my dress. The boy takes a burlap bag lying near us and wraps it around me.

I want to leave this frightening person, but I don't want it to be found out that I don't have a ticket and be thrown off the ship, especially since I've gotten this far into the journey. I also don't want life to become more dangerous being atop the deck with this strange boy. "Maybe he isn't so bad after all," I think, for he has given me the burlap bag for warmth.

"I have a plan. There are so many dying and thirsting in the hold, including my own family, and there are casks of water and savory dishes in the captain's quarters. Why should we suffer while the captain and his mistress are kept fat and healthy?" the boy says to me.

I look at him again. What does he want from me? Maggie and I have gotten our allotted share of food because we are still considered children. It isn't much and we always want more, but at least it's keeping us alive until we arrive in America. There are some adults who have to go without food on some days. Worse than that, water is being deprived us, for there's little left due to a leakage, and there are so many people with the ship fever who seem to require more than usual.

The boy continues, "I've a key I took off the hook in the captain's quarters when they were out and no one was watching. We need to get inside while they sleep and take some food for the people below. I can't carry it alone and I know you have a kind heart, for I saw you giving your food away when we first boarded."

"I'll not be stealing!" I say too loudly, surprised that this unusual boy has been watching me ever since I've been secretly hiding in the dresser.

"Shhh!" he whispers, pushing me to the floor and sitting down beside me. "It's not considered stealing to share with our own people who will perish unless we do!"

I know there are people dying but not so much from the lack of food. It's the fever and how it comes upon them so suddenly that is killing them. There have been two new cases of this strange fever and the poor creatures in the hold are in a shocking state. The captain's wife, the mistress, is down in the hold daily administering a few drops of laudanum to give them some relief from their suffering. This is a remedy to help them sleep but she says it can be deadly if it isn't used with caution. I heard the mate say to the captain that there are only enough provisions for another week, and surely it will take at least two more weeks to arrive in America.

"I'll not steal from the good mistress who is doing her best to care for us!" I tell this evil boy.

"The good mistress is fat as a cow, and it's her job to be down in the hold helping the sick!" the boy says. "It won't do her and the captain any good to own a ship that carries the dead to shore."

"Tell me your name," I demand of him, replacing my fear with boldness.

"My name's Jack, and I know your name is Nora," he says.

"How would you know? Did the fairies tell you?" I tease him.

"I know because I've a mind to watch all the passengers closely. I keep a journal and write everything down. I heard your sister calling your name."

"You know how to read and write?" I ask with wonder. I have only begun to learn but it's a terrible struggle for me. My family usually speaks and writes in Irish in our home. The schools teach us our studies in English, and I haven't been doing well learning it, either. A few books in Irish have been left for the O'Connors and I pleaded with Mam to take them with us on this journey and not give them away. I'm as hungry to read as I am to eat, and here is this strange boy who can read! I love the smell of books and the feel of clothbound covers. Just touching them and picking out a few words makes me feel important and wise.

"I know how to read and write, and I can help you learn if you help me get the food from the captain's quarters," Jack answers.

"Do you think it right to steal?" I ask.

"Only to help someone who is more desperate than the person you are stealing from," Jack replies.

"I don't feel good about it," I say.

"I promise to take all the blame if we're found out," Jack says.

"It might be found out that I have never had a ticket. If they do another roll call, my name won't be on it," I say, realizing that being caught would be worse than Jack being caught.

"The captain wouldn't be throwing a child into the sea for not having a ticket," Jack says with a chuckle. "It isn't just that . . . I don't know . . . It's like I feel the eyes of God piercing my soul all the time."

"Then He'll be proud of you to be helping the dying on this ship!"

And so it is that Jack and I devise a plan to slip into the captain's cabin. We will take some provisions that have been stored there and give them to the hungry and sick people in the hold. I'm in disbelief that I've agreed to help Jack steal food from the captain's quarters. I guess it's because I sense in Jack that he's a good soul and that we are on an important mission. Besides, he can read and he has promised to teach me. By the time we arrive in America, I will be able to read!

Chapter Sixteen

ADVENTURE WITH A NEW FRIEND

Morning arrived hours ago, but not in the hold of the *Star*. There is no light and the people huddle in filth and despair around me. I have nearly become accustomed to the sounds of their wailing and weeping for water. Maggie and I have remained healthy, though we are feeble and thin. Everyone is dispirited because the journey has become longer than expected and we are running out of food and water. There's a cloud of melancholy and sickness that hangs over the whole ship.

"Coming down, coming down!" shouts a sailor descending into the hold. He climbs down with a hose to spray out the hold with water.

"You're making matters worse than they are down here!" one of the passengers yells.

Maggie and I grab our things and put them in the dresser. Then we stand in front of it to guard it from being sprayed with water from the sailor's hose.

There is so much foulness and dirt in the hold because we don't have the means or the strength to keep it clean. We do the best we can, going to the deck once a week to wash, but now there are so many sick with the fever that they can only lie in unsanitary conditions because they are unable to care for themselves. I think that this method used by the sailors is a desperate attempt to alleviate some of the terrible conditions, but it only causes agitation amongst all of us. Our few belongings have become soggy and Maggie says it creates a steam bath for more disease to spread.

After this disturbing episode, I look into the dresser. I want to check on the food Jack and I have stolen from the captain's cabin. I can't fit into the dresser for there is so much food! I've had to sleep on the bunk with Maggie and the wee one from the family above us ever since Jack and I took the food from the captain's quarters. I have stashed it in every corner and Jack has stored some in another place on the ship. I am waiting for Jack to signal to me when it is time to begin passing it out down in the hold. Jack has managed to haul a whole cask of water from the depot and store it under the bunk where he and his family are sleeping. Jack has a mother, father, and three sisters. One of his sisters is suffering from the early stages of the fever.

"What are you looking for in the dresser now, girl?" Maggie asks.

"Nothing, Maggie," I reply.

"I know you're holding out on me, Nora, and you haven't been sleeping in the dresser. I know you are up to something. I feel it in my bones. You must tell me, for you are my charge, and besides, I take great responsibility in caring for you."

"You don't have to take care of me, Maggie, and you know it. You're just plain nosy!" I say, somewhat in jest.

"All we've been through on this ship, and now you're keeping secrets from me," Maggie answers back with a pouting face.

I am finding it very difficult to keep what Jack and I have done from Maggie. "You've got to promise me, Maggie, not to utter a word to anyone. If you do, I might get thrown overboard."

"What have you done, Nora?"

I open the door of the dresser and motion for Maggie to look in. Maggie looks in at a large block of Cheshire cheese, dried herrings, and piles of biscuits. There are also jars of preserves and some whiskey as well. I've been hiding this food for two days now and it is beginning to smell stronger than the dirty stench of the hold.

"Oh, Nora, where did you get so much food? Not from the fairies this time, I'll gather!"

"Shhh, don't talk so loud! As soon as Jack comes below, we're going to pass it out to everyone here in the hold. There won't be a crumb left in the dresser, but we'll manage to hide some preserves and biscuits for ourselves, I promise you that, Maggie. No one will suspect us, Jack and me, stealing from the captain's cabin," I confess.

Maggie is shocked and begins fumbling with the food in the dresser, all the while shaking her head.

"Nora, what have you done! They have the food counted in the captain's room and they'll find out about you and this Jack, who must have put you up to this criminal act. Oh, Nora, you'll be thrown out to sea! I can't bear to lose you, Nora. You've become my only family!" Maggie begins crying and covers her face with her hands.

A twinge of guilt comes over me, but I quickly dismiss it with thoughts of how happy the people in the hold are going to be when they are able to eat such delicious food. After Jack and I pass out the food to everyone in the hold, I'm going to go to the priest during the evening prayers and confess my sin of stealing. I'm convinced that I'm doing the right thing, but the stealing part of it does bother me very much. For that, I will need forgiveness.

"I'll not watch it happen, Nora, and I'll have no part in it! I'm going to walk upon the deck until it is all over, and when they throw the two of you into the sea, I'll turn my head! Oh, I can't bear it, Nora!" Maggie exclaims with tears running down her face. Then she leaves the bunk and climbs the stairs to the deck in a flash. I call after her but she ignores me. I have to let her go because I must find Jack to find out when we will pass out the food before someone finds us out.

While Jack and I are busy feeding the poor people in the hold with the captain's food, Maggie went to the deck and encountered the handsome young man who helped us with the dresser at the beginning of our trip. As Maggie peered over the side of the deck, the sea was as sparkling glass and a lovely clear, green hue. There were only a few people walking about, but they appeared lost in thought. Maggie closed her eyes for a few moments. Then she heard someone yelling out nearby her.

"Beware of death! I saw it with my own eyes, I did. I saw it!" cried out a frail-looking boy standing with his father a few feet away from Maggie.

"Hush, son," his father said.

"I saw a shark, Da. Isn't a shark a sign of death?" he asked.

"There's nothing a shark can do to hurt us, son, not if we are in the boat and he is in the sea," replied the boy's father.

Maggie knew the boy and his father because the mother died a few days ago from the fever. She had been ill for two weeks and suffered immensely. In good health, the woman had been beautiful, but when she died, she had been unrecognizable. When she was dying, her poor husband stood by her holding a candle in his hand, awaiting the departure of her spirit. After she died, he and the priest had muttered prayers over her enshrouded body as it was lowered into the ocean for a burial. Maggie and I had watched in horror, fearful that one day we, too, would die in such a lonely and terrible manner.

Maggie also had to console me because I was thinking of my family as I watched this grave event.
Maggie told me to put it out of my mind that maybe
on another ship following the *Star* across the sea,
my family was dying and being buried in the sea.
Maggie and I had been praying every night for each
member of my family, but we also knew that many
of those who had died had probably also prayed to
live. It was peace then we had to ask for because
the dying would soon not have anymore suffering.
Only peace. The night of this woman's terrifying
death, Maggie had cradled me in her arms while I
wept.

"Excuse me, Miss Maggie. It is Maggie, isn't it?"
the handsome young gentleman asked Maggie.

Maggie was startled, for she was lost in her
thoughts about me as she looked out at the sea. "Oh,
yes, I'm Maggie. Oh, it's you!" she said awkwardly, and
then blushed.

"It's Margaret, sir. Margaret O'Houlihan, but certainly you may call me Maggie. Nora and I . . . well,
Nora is doing . . . Well, sir, never mind me, I'm a bit
worn out and worried," Maggie says, thinking only of
my plight if I am caught with the food. Then poor
Maggie slumped down onto a trunk used to store extra ropes, and sighed.

"I want to help you and your sister," the young
man said to Maggie. "I know what your sister and Jack
have done. The captain and the mistress are so busy
tending the sick and dying on this ship, they haven't
yet noticed the food has been taken. The reason I
know about it is because there have been other passengers complaining about their meager provisions.
They've been walking back and forth in front of the
captain's cabin waiting to steal food. I've had to keep
a watch for the captain and I saw Nora and Jack steal
the food in the night. I didn't want to apprehend them,

for I knew the captain would awaken, and who knows what might have happened to them. I thought I might find you today and ask you to convince the two children to return the food or else their lives may be in jeopardy."

"You don't think the captain would throw the two children overboard, do you, sir?" Maggie asked the gentleman.

"I can't imagine he would, Maggie, but then again, times are difficult and people are desperate. The captain is anxious and overcome with all the people who are ill with the fever. Many are dying and there aren't enough provisions and water to finish this journey. Once again, the English have not managed their ships well, nor provided for the people they cast onto them!"

"Nora won't listen to me. I tried talking to her this morning. For all I know, she and Jack have already given the food away to everyone in the hold," Maggie told him.

"Then we'll go right now and try to stop them!" the young man said as he helped Maggie to her feet.

"What is your name, sir?" Maggie asked as she looked into the eyes of this intriguing, handsome man. Her heart began to unfold some of its dreams that had been tucked away since the Famine came to Ireland.

"My name is Robert, and I'm a cleric and a writer. You can be sure this tragic and eventful voyage will be someday written about," he said, his eyes full of compassion.

As Maggie and Robert climbed down into the hold, Robert took his handkerchief from his pocket and held it over his nose. He, in fact, had not been in the hold except once, and that was only at the beginning of the journey. He was shocked by the stench and filth that emanated from the living quarters of the Irish passengers. He could barely stand it and climbed back to the deck. Maggie scrambled up after him and realized uncomfortably that she herself must smell for being so long down in the hold.

Robert coughed and faced the sea. Maggie stood behind him wondering what she was to do. She didn't know if she should go back into the hold and attempt to get the food back without him or ask him what to do next.

After moments passed, Robert turned to Maggie. "Let's go down now, Maggie. I didn't realize how terrible it has gotten in the hold. I've been staying in the captain's quarters and though the mistress goes there every day, she has never confided in me. I'm so sorry, Maggie, I didn't really know what deplorable conditions you all have been living in!"

Maggie and Robert went down into the hold, but Jack and I had already passed out the food taken from the captain's cabin. Everyone in the hold had been given some food, even though many were delirious and couldn't eat even a crumb. It didn't stop Jack and me from trying to help them. We left the food sitting on people's sickbeds anyway. There was a man in one of the bunks who had died the night before, and his corpse was next to his wife, who was in the last stages of the fever herself. I was so sad, but I was also no longer shocked by seeing death. I motioned for Jack to give the wife some water. I then made the sign of the cross and went on to the next bunk. When we finished passing out all the food, I said goodbye to Jack and climbed to the deck to look for the priest. My guilt for stealing was now more than I could stand, even though I also felt proud of myself for feeding the people. I felt strong and enormously different from the girl who first cowered in fear when climbing into the dresser to begin this journey.

"Father Boyle, Father Boyle!" I cry out when I find him, "I need you to hear my confession, please Father!"

Father Boyle is just recuperating from the fever himself and is weak and tired.

"Not now, child, not now. I've only to become stronger and then I can resume my duties," he states.

"No, Father!" I plead. "I need forgiveness now!" and then I slump down upon the deck, my fears beginning to overtake me again, just like in Ireland. My newfound mantle of strength and determination to do what I did with Jack must not have become a real part of me. I fear I will die without the priest's forgiveness. And I might really die, I think, for when I'm found out to have stolen food and to be without a proper ticket, I'll be thrown overboard. I need this priest to make me right with God before it happens!

I can tell that Father Boyle is interested in my determination to be forgiven. He tells me that life has gotten so out of kilter it doesn't matter that confession is heard for every little thing. He sits down next to me and takes my hands into his and prays over me. When it's time for me to confess, I blurt out, "I robbed the captain!"

"Oh, child, this is a serious crime, and you've put me in a difficult position. If you choose, I'll take you to the captain and you can tell him the truth. God will forgive you, it's true, but you must live up to what you've done," Father Boyle says.

I stand up as soon as the priest finishes praying for me. I thank him and run away from him down into the hold, for I do not want to be dragged before the captain. Now that I have God's forgiveness, I must fight for my life as much as possible, for I dearly need to see my Da and Mam and sisters again! Jack is nowhere in sight, for he is hiding somewhere on the ship. He hasn't even told me where he is hiding but said he'd stay there until we reach America. He took enough water and food with him to live on. I have only one place to go, and that, of course, is the dresser.

I climb into the dresser to hide, and when I do, I find a note written in Irish and some food from Jack: "Thanks to my new friend, Nora, who has helped me give love and food to the people on the *Star*. Their suffering is lessened because of you. Until we meet again in America, Love, Jack."

I'm exhausted from this experience that has taken me on a journey within myself that feels as rigorous as the journey across the sea. I can't think any further about right and wrong, and fall into a deep sleep in the dresser. I don't awaken until Maggie, the captain, Robert, and Father Boyle knock on the dresser and tell me to come out.

Chapter Seventeen

FORGIVENESS

"Nora," Maggie says as she opens the door of the dresser, "Nora, wake up!"

I stir from a deep sleep, and immediately remember the stark truth of my deeds. I climb out of the dresser and look into the faces of the captain and Father Boyle, and my tears begin to flow. All around me, people are getting off their bunks and coming to stand by me while I weep before the stern captain. They begin to shout in Irish at the captain that he must let me stay on board in my dresser.

"Please, everyone, return to your bunks immediately!" the captain speaks loudly to the crowd. "This child shall be spared. I know your grievances and we're about to embark upon a remedy to alleviate some of the hunger and thirst you are all suffering from. Please be patient. This child has done wrong, as well as her young partner, Jack, but we'll be charitable towards them."

I am relieved by this kindhearted decision of the captain. I have received the priest's prayers for forgiveness and now I am forgiven by the captain. I will not die after all! I have such mixed feelings about what I have done. I know stealing is a sin, but I also know that the people in the bunks have been suffering. I hug Maggie tightly around her neck and we both fall over onto the bunk. Then I get up and stand

125

in front of the captain with the little courage I still carry within me.

"Please, sir, I'm very sorry for breaking into your cabin, but I didn't do it for myself . . . Jack and I did it to help all these people," I say as my arms sweep across the room, encompassing all those I had given food to who are healthy enough to stand by me.

I look at the captain and his face shows warmth and concern. I don't think he could really throw any child overboard, for he is a compassionate man. Maggie had told me, however, that there are such captains who wouldn't blink an eye in doing so for a lesser crime than mine and Jack's.

"You did wrong, Nora," the captain says to me. "I have not been hoarding food and supplies, except perhaps the preserves that my wife has put up for our private use. We are to be at sea still for some time and we are running short of provisions. The mate and I have been rationing the food, not out of selfishness, but for all your own good. Do you know how grave an act this is which you have done, Nora, for there is little food left for the rest of our journey!"

When I hear these stern words, I'm stunned. I hang my head in shame and understand for the first time the folly of my act. I am but a child and I thought I knew better than the captain of his ship! Though I believe Jack was right when he told me that many captains starve the people on their ships, this captain is not one of those. Jack also told me that the captains must follow English laws for taking passengers across the sea, and the allotment for provisions is never sufficient for the passengers. I have heard the mate say that the *Star* was really built for carrying only two hundred people, but there are three hundred of us packed into it! It's a wonder it hasn't sunk! And now because of what I have done, the people I thought I was helping might end up worse off than they were!

"I know you meant well, Nora, but without under-
standing the situation, what you meant for good has
turned to evil. We'll be at sea without enough food!"
the captain states to me. "It will take a miracle to get
us to port alive!"

"Then I'll pray for one, sir, and if I cause the death
of anyone, I'll never be able to stand it!" I sob again
and throw myself onto Maggie. Maggie wraps her arms
around me and holds me. Many of the passengers try
to comfort me, and after everyone leaves, I climb back
into the dresser. That evening there's a fair wind and
the *Star* is much quieter than it has ever been since
leaving Ireland.

One morning, a week later, gloom spreads over
the *Star* by impenetrable fog, and the sound of the
foghorn is dismal and foreboding. Delirious passengers moan loudly in terrible pain. Maggie and I stay in
our bunk praying and listening to the moans and
wretchedness around us.

Later in the day, we climb the steps to the deck
and find a tub of dirty water to wash in, our stomachs
knotted with hunger. Maggie has dry heaves and becomes sick over the railing. I rub her back and try to
console her. Both of us sit down on some empty casks
that had once held water.

The mate walks over to us. "The captain and the
mistress are mixing some seawater with gruel, and it
will be served to the passengers. Are you strong enough
to help serve the passengers?"

"Surely we'll be strong to help, sir, but we need to
take some food ourselves," Maggie answers.

"You'll be the first to eat," he says, and is off. The
mate is a good fellow, and has never questioned
whether I have a ticket to be on board. In fact, there
hasn't been a roll call in a long time. The mate is a
hard-working sailor, and he's one minute in the hold
waiting on a dying patient, and in the next minute,
stretched across the ship, reefing a topsail.

After Maggie and I take some nourishment, we assist the mate, along with Robert who has also come to help. We give the awful tasting gruel to the passengers in the hold who are unable to come to the deck to eat it. I'm thankful to be able to give food to the people I'm afraid I may cause to die because of stealing their food and giving it to them all at once. I think of Jack and wonder if I should try to find him to tell him we were wrong in what we did, but I don't have time.

We finish our duties, and then we are lying on our bunks resting and talking about America, when Robert comes to us.

"Please come up to the deck, for I have terrible news to share with you," he tells us. Maggie is nervous being around Robert, her face red from blushing as she tries to fix her hair that is matted and dirty.

We sit on top of the deck with the fog still thick enough to cut with a knife.

"It's about Jack. He took sick with the fever and came out of hiding last night. He died early this morning. He didn't suffer long. He was sick only a few hours and then fell silent. Shortly after, he died in his mother's arms. The mistress and his mother nursed him well and gave him great comfort during his last hours."

"No, you are telling me a lie to punish me!" I scream at Robert.

"Nora, Jack was forgiven as you have been for stealing the food. There is no punishment. In fact, the captain has honored him by giving him one of his medals, which poor Jack held on to when he died. I'm sorry, Nora, to have to tell you this. But there is something Jack also wanted me to share with you. He told me to tell you that you should not ever be fearful, for there will always be angels close by. These were his words for you, Nora," Robert says as I cry on Maggie's shoulder.

There is no consoling me for the rest of the day. I climb into the dresser and stay there. I don't want to come out again until we reach America. I don't even feel hungry anymore. My hunger pains have left me, or else they're now hidden under the sorrow I feel for Jack. I want my Mam's arms and Da's fiddle playing. I want Kate's comforting words, and I even miss Meg's scolding. When I close my eyes to try and feel my family's love surrounding me, I don't feel it as I used to feel, and I fear that they, too, must have died on another ship from the fever. Soon I tire from my grief and fall asleep. As I sleep, the dresser becomes my sanctuary and comfort, and it is there I find the strength to go on.

Chapter Eighteen

HOPE

"Nora . . . wake up . . . there's someone here to visit you." Maggie's voice penetrates my sleep and causes me to wake with a start. I don't want to wake up, for I'm afraid of finding out about another tragedy!

I sit up in the dresser and bump my head. Then the pain of knowing that Jack is gone comes back to me. I rub my head and come out of the dresser. Standing before me is a woman with two small girls clutching her skirts.

"Ye must be the one Jack talked of. Ye must be Nora," says the woman. "I'm Jack's mammy, and he asked me to give you this." The woman held out something wrapped in a piece of cloth. I take it, unwrap it, and find a cloth journal with colorful and intricate designs sewn on its cover. I touch it, feeling its texture and marveling at the artwork.

"It's Jack's words," his mam says, as tears flow down her face. "Jack loved words, and when he learned to read and write, he never stopped writing on anything he could find. His schoolmaster gave him this writing book awhile back. Jack no more had to write on the flat stones he'd find around the fields. Will you take good care of it for him, Nora? He told me you loved words, too."

"I'll treasure it, to be sure, and it'll never be far from me," I say as my tears fall freely. This time I'm not ashamed of them. I give Jack's mammy a long hug and she leaves me alone with the journal.

I spend the rest of the day trying to decipher Jack's writing in his journal. I am determined to learn how to read every word when I arrive in America. America! Is it really true we will be there soon? Will I find my family? Will we all live long enough to see the shores of this promised land Aunt Bridget raved about in her letters? That evening, Maggie and I go up to the deck for the evening prayers with Father Boyle.

Afterwards, we want to see if there might be something cooking in the fireboxes, but the fires haven't been started, and the pots and pans are empty. Some of the passengers stand silently looking out to sea. There is a brilliant sunset, and the water is still. I've never seen the sea so still. Suddenly, sleek porpoises burst through the calm waters and splash playfully before our ship. Then there are dolphins rolling over one another as if to entertain all of us bedraggled travelers. We begin to clap and yell for joy. Maggie and I are in awe as we watch the glorious show before us. It goes on for a number of minutes and then stops. Then it is quiet again and no one moves or utters a word for many moments.

"Look!" shouts an old man, "Look over there! There are pools of fish!"

"I see thousands of fish!" shouts a child.

"Are they eatin' fish?" asks a woman.

The captain and his mate have heard the jubilation and come to the deck to see what is going on. They, too, are surprised by all the fish surrounding the *Star*.

"Well, glory to God," the captain says, "I never saw so many mackerel in all my sailing days! Grab some lines, everyone, let's fish!"

We all begin to make homemade fishing lines out of anything we can find. We pull the thread out of some of Maggie's dresses, double it, and then take a hook off a dress, and turn it into a fishhook. There are so many mackerel that Maggie and I catch fifty in an hour! The captain has captured enough to fill a barrel. Fires are started, and there is rejoicing and laughter amongst us. We who have become so weary and hungry have been given a miracle. Only God knows how many of us had stood alongside the railing of the deck that evening contemplating jumping overboard.

Within the next few days, however, more people perish from the effects of the fever. The ship is a pest-ridden, disease-ridden, and putrid floating mess. Those who are healthy, such as Maggie, Robert, the mistress and I, nurse and console the sick and dying. People aren't shocked by death anymore. Some of them lose their minds and sit on their bunks without memory, and sometimes people begin screaming and running up and down the deck. But many of the Irish passengers are filled with hope after the spectacular display of marine life that was followed by fish being multiplied before our eyes.

"There's dancin' on the deck! There's dancin' on the deck!" shout a few passengers one night. These are passengers who have recovered from the fever and are unable to refrain from the joy of having survived an unforgettable ordeal. Everyone who is able climbs to the deck and joins in the recreation. Maggie and I have been sitting on our bunk talking again about what we are going to do in America when we finally arrive. I ask Maggie to stay with me and my family, but as much as Maggie wants to be with me forever, she tells me that she doesn't want to become a burden.

"No, Nora, it wouldn't be right for us being such friends and all, and then me becoming an employee of your family."

"Maggie, don't be silly, you wouldn't be our employee, for we'd never have the money to hire you. But you must stay with us while you find work. Wouldn't it be lovely for all of us to be together? You must promise me that you'll not favor my two sisters because they're older. You must admit that I'm probably the best friend you've ever had in your life!"

"Nora, dear Nora, I've grown into a woman, I think, just caring for you!" Maggie says with a giggle as she tousles my hair that is dirty and hasn't been plaited for weeks.

"Let's go upstairs and do a jig!" she says, pulling me up the stairs to the deck.

Maggie and I dance until the moon seems to be smiling over us and the stars drip a silver lining into our dreams. It doesn't seem to matter to any of us that we are really too weak for such dancing, because strength comes into our frail bodies when we hear the music. The fiddler is accompanied by no other musician but the stamping of feet in perfect time with his music. It is a sight to behold to see the energy and the indomitable spirit in all of us as we display our flair and talent for the dancing. Before calling it a night and descending the stairs to the hold, Maggie and I stop at the tub to wash the sweat that has accumulated on us while dancing.

"It's another wonder, Maggie! Look . . . look . . . into the sky above us!" I cry out. The fiddler stops playing, feet stop dancing, and everyone's heads turn towards the sky.

Radiant meteors are celebrating life with us as we dance. They are prancing about in wild playfulness above the *Star*. There are sighs and exclamations of joy as life outside the boat interacts with life in the boat, and gives us strength to survive the rest of our journey.

"It's as if the stars are dancing with us to our own music and feet!" I exclaim. "Is it a sign, dear Maggie? Is it a sign?" I ask.

"'Tis, dear Nora, 'tis," Maggie says as she hugs me close to her while we sit upon burlap bags and gaze at the show in the sky.

Chapter Nineteen

ALMOST AMERICA

More days pass. It is the morning of the festival of St. John, a Catholic holiday, and everyone is hoping to see land. There is an increase to the names upon the sick roll, and Maggie and I never have time to rest as we care for and comfort the ill passengers. When we are finally able to go to bed late at night, we are awakened by someone needing us. We see frightening episodes of death, but mostly peaceful departures amongst the dying. Maggie and I don't have time to become bewildered, and before fear grips us, there is yet another patient to tend to. We weep over the children who are left without parents. If these children survive, they will end up in orphanages in America.

One morning I wake up early with a terrible pain in my head. It feels as if my head is going to burst and I cannot open my eyes without worse pain. I cry for Maggie to help me and she opens the door of the dresser.

"It feels as if my head is going to come off my shoulders!" I say to her.

Maggie goes to the deck to find some water for me. The only water that is left is being mixed with seawater. By the time she returns to me, I am lying on the bunk tossing and moaning. "It's come to me, too, Maggie! It's come and I don't want to die without seeing my family again!"

"No, Nora, my pet. You'll not die. You'll come through this fever, you will. I know it," Maggie says, but I see the same sorrow in her face that is there when we watch a passenger with the fever take their last breath.

Maggie gives me sips of water. "Nora, think of the ones we've been caring for. The ones with the worst fevers overcame it."

"If I die, Maggie, tell my family everything. Tell them I love them and how strong I've become."

Maggie continues to comfort me, giving me sips of water and rubbing my forehead. When I finally doze off to sleep, Maggie leaves me to find the mistress.

"I can't tell if she'll recover. I just can't, Maggie. I'm weary with so much sickness on this ship, but we'll give her everything we can to try to get her through it," the mistress tells her.

Later I awaken and cry out again, "My head, give me something for my head!"

The only remedy the mistress has is a little brandy to help me sleep. As soon as I swallow it, I doze again.

"Keep putting cold cloths on her head and give her some liquid. And when she can't sleep, we'll have to dispense the laudanum to her," the mistress instructs Maggie.

"There's little liquid left and I think the seawater isn't good for her," Maggie says.

"I've brought you something from Robert for her," the mistress says as she hands her a bottle of lime juice. "It's mixed with a little sugar. Let her drink it in sips when she wakes."

"Give Robert my thanks, ma'am, and tell him to be praying for Nora," Maggie tells the mistress with a sparkle in her eyes when she mentions his name.

Maggie cares for me as best as she is able, but we both struggle to believe I will make it. There have been so many others we have cared for whose symptoms are similar to mine. I know Maggie is trying to fight her despairing thoughts and she tends to me like a loving mother hour after hour. I don't think anymore about living or dying. I'm delirious and when I sleep, I dream of Ireland and Miss Maggie, cowslips in my plaited hair, and the Cake we celebrated before the Famine came to destroy our lives. Many of the other passengers come by to see if they can help, and those who are also sick with the fever, ask for me every day.

A few days later, the *Star* travels full sail at eight knots an hour and passes some small islands with swarms of gannets flying about. The *Star* is getting close to its destination, and the atmosphere aboard the ship becomes excitable. Everyone is clamoring to clean the hold and themselves in order to pass the inspection when they reach the quarantine island. How long the ship will have to stay in quarantine depends upon the state of the passengers in the hold. It is excruciating for the captain to exact work from the sick and weary, whose water supply has dwindled to nothing. He is waiting for another ship to come along and give them a cask or two to hold them over until they get into port.

In the afternoon, the *Star* begins passing a number of fishing boats, anchored at varying intervals to catch cod fish. The captain tries to make contact with one of them to learn the bearings of land. He is finally able to speak with the captain on a wherry that is carrying cattle and he finds out that the *Star* is nearing New York. He discovers that they have to stop at Staten Island, the designated quarantine station for any ship arriving from Ireland and England. Then the *Star* will go into the South Street Quay to deliver the Irish passengers to their promised land.

Maggie tells me that cheers erupt amongst some of the passengers sitting on the deck. It's a sunny and humid day, and there is great anticipation everywhere.

"Take me aboard!" cries the captain of the wherry. The captain of the *Star* is reluctant to let him on ship, for he knows he will be shocked by the sickness on board.

"Do you have a cask of water we can have? We've run out, mate. The want of pure water has afflicted my passengers," our captain says.

"I'll gladly give you one," the captain of the wherry says, and cheers of delight break out again amongst the people standing on deck.

When the cask is delivered, and the captain of the wherry has seen the state of the *Star*, he is sorry he has come aboard. He soon departs and the cask of water lasts until the *Star* arrives on Staten Island.

By evening of the next day, the *Star* is on the north side of the island and the passengers can almost touch the trees on the bank. There is a pink sunset illuminating the hope felt in the passengers' hearts waiting to touch their new land.

The *Star* is anchored all night and into the next morning. The poor passengers are anxious and can't understand why the *Star* doesn't dock and allow them to set foot on their longed-for destination. The captain, mistress, mate, and Robert are very uneasy as well, for all the food is gone, except for some dried herring that they try to divvy up amongst the passengers. The *Star* sits before the quarantine station on Staten Island and waits for the inspecting physician to arrive and give permission to lay anchor at the island. The next morning passes, and then the next. The passengers are in disbelief over being within reach of help, and yet neglected and helpless in their new country.

Meanwhile, the mate's wife becomes ill with the fever, and passes away. The mate grieves so terribly, he is unable to attend to his duties. The effects of the fever do not abate, and the cries of the suffering continue. I am lingering near death with the debilitating effects of the fever, and I hardly know we're near our destination.

One day, at last, there can be seen coming across the ocean a boat with four oars and a steersman, carrying the inspecting physician. The doctor comes on deck and inquires of the captain about the condition of the passengers.

"How many patients are there at present?" he asks. When the captain replies with the number of deaths and the number of the sick, the doctor states that there are almost fifty of the same ships floating with corpses and pestilence surrounding the island. He indicates that only the healthy passengers will be able to leave, and a boat will be sent for them shortly. The ill passengers will have to wait to go to Staten Island to the quarantine hospital when beds become available. He tells the captain that the hospital is currently full of other passengers who came to America with the fever.

"I am sorry to say that there are no more hospital beds available on the island, Captain," the physician says.

"You don't understand, Doctor, we can't endure another day or another night without provisions—food and medicine. We are out of everything, and more will die if they aren't tended to," the captain states firmly.

The physician snatches up his hat, takes the information he has written down, and hastily leaves the *Star*. Some of the passengers begin cursing the physician and try to get into the boat he is leaving in. The oarsmen beat back their dire attempts, and the boat sails quickly away from the *Star*.

"You must sail right to the island, anyway, Captain. The physician is just one man, and he can't understand the desperation our journey has brought to us!" a passenger shouts.

"No, I cannot disobey orders," replies the captain. With that answer, a few of the men who are pale and walking bags of bones, fall upon the captain and try to beat him.

"We'll take over this boat, then! We've had enough!" they cry, and attempt to beat the captain with their fists, which have very little skin on them. They can wait no longer for the mercy of God, nor the mercy of man. More men begin to gather to fight upon the deck of the *Star*. The passengers are so close to paradise, and yet still so far away.

Chapter Twenty

THE END AND THE BEGINNING

Robert and the mistress fire the blunderbuss, and the fighting ceases. The captain is taken to his cabin, his wounds are cleaned and bandaged. He is given laudanum to induce sleep, for he is agitated and overcome with exhaustion. He has not suffered much, for the men who attacked him had been too weak to inflict serious injury. They, in fact, are ashamed of themselves, and are working hard to gain the forgiveness of the crew. Others who had gotten involved stated that they were only trying to stop the attack. Overall, it didn't turn out as terrible as it could have been. A more crucial dilemma remains. How will the sick passengers be cared for? How will family members be separated from one another when it comes time for the healthy ones to be taken to shore? The mistress and Robert talk of what should be done.

"You and the captain go and find some rest on land, mistress. I'll stay and watch over the ship. There must be health officials who will come on board and give their assistance while the patients wait for hospital beds," Robert says.

"The captain will never leave his ship, Robert. You go and assist those leaving, especially the pretty lass with the dark hair and blue eyes," the mistress says with a twinkle in her eyes.

Maggie pleads with them to take me ashore with her, but they're afraid that if I am moved, I will die.

"The child, Nora, will not be able to go," Robert says, realizing with sadness the impact it will have on Maggie.

"The child, Nora, might not live, Robert, and Maggie will not leave her side," the mistress says.

"Nora will not survive if she stays any longer in the hold without help. Maggie cannot care for her anymore. And the physician will not allow any of the healthy ones to stay on board with the sick," Robert says.

"Our Nora might not have long for this world," the mistress says sadly. She cannot imagine me perishing after all I've been through, but she has seen the same death grip on the ill passengers who died from this fever. She wonders at why she herself has not taken ill, being that she is an old woman and has been going without sleep and proper nourishment.

The next morning, boats arrive, as promised, to carry only those passengers who are well, or who have recuperated from the fever, to the coveted shore of America. It will be a few hours and these Irish emigrants will finally place their feet upon their new country's soil. Ireland's sufferings have grown dim in their minds, but Ireland's beauty still beats strongly in their hearts. Onward to the South Street Quay in New York City they will go, not knowing how little their difficulties will lessen.

The crew who arrives to take the passengers ashore is very demanding. They possess little patience for the weak and slow-moving emigrants leaving the *Star*.

"There are vast numbers of sick in the hospitals and in tents upon the island, and already, many nuns and clergymen, as well as doctors, have gotten the fever. Your boat is not as unfortunate as many we've seen. Those ships are laden with cargoes of the dead! They never stop arriving! So move yourselves quickly!" shouts one crewman. It is obvious that the terror of the fever and the sight of so much suffering has hardened them and made them insensitive to the passengers from the *Star*.

A husband, the only support for his gaunt and ill wife and children, is forcibly torn away from them. There are shrieks of protest as mothers are dragged away from their sick children.

"When your family recovers, you'll see them again," a crewman shouts. Everyone weeps bitterly, including the mistress, Robert, and the crew.

Then up from the hold appears a lovely young woman, dressed in a long frilly dress, though it is quite soiled. She is much too thin due to her ordeal on this Irish coffin ship for over three months. It is Maggie, and she is quickly examined for signs of the fever, and though she is pale and feeble, she is pushed ahead to board the boat to carry her to the island.

"Not without my dresser!" she suddenly shouts to everyone around her.

"Now, Maggie, please, there is hardly enough room on the boat to take the passengers . . . ," Robert interjects, quickly going to her side. Was he not at her side so long ago at the beginning of this journey?

Tears begin flowing down Maggie's white porcelain cheeks. The crew looks on with impatience, and one of them responds. "Where is this dresser, then?" he asks.

"It's below in the hold," Maggie says, looking sorrowfully towards the hold, and then at Robert, who looks at her assuredly.

"I'll be glad to assist this young lady with her lovely dresser, sir," he says. "In fact, I'll disburse funds for the dresser to be delivered safely with this young woman."

Maggie's pale cheeks blossom with color while Robert and a crewman climb down into the stinking hold to gather the very heavy dresser and secure its place upon the boat.

None of the other passengers utters a word, for they know just how precious the dresser has become to Maggie, as it has also become precious to them as well.

While the boats rock and tarry upon the Atlantic sea, so near the dream of happiness and safety in a new land, there is immense sorrow over the loss of life, loss of family members, and the loss of their country.

Maggie stays with the dresser, never letting it out of her sight. She rubs the pine wood that seems to breathe with memories of hope and love, as well as loss. Great loss! What will her new life be like in New York City that is so unlike Ireland! How will she survive?

It is only when the boat, at last, arrives upon the rich soil of America, that Maggie unties the straps on the dresser and opens the cupboard.

"Nora . . . Nora, dear, wake up and be well, for we are in America!"

Epilogue

Nora survived the fever. The fever had begun to abate the day before the boats arrived to take the healthy to shore. By the day of departure, it was believed her fever had left her, though she was unable to lift her head off the floor of the dresser by herself and she wouldn't be allowed to leave the *Star*. The captain, his mistress, Robert, and Maggie decided that Nora should hide in the dresser while it was placed on the boat to carry the healthy passengers to shore. Through many dangers on shore and with Robert's help, Maggie was able to find out where Nora's Aunt Bridget lived. Aunt Bridget and Maggie nursed Nora back to health in the loud, bustling, and boisterous city of New York. One of the neighbors in a large tenement house that Aunt Bridget lived in brought her a beautiful calico kitten to help her while she convalesced. She named him Paws and he became her best friend, except for Maggie, of course. Paws loved to curl up in the dresser and sleep. Every night since their difficult arrival in America, Nora and Paws would curl up in the dresser with Jack's journal, Nora clutching her Da's coin to her heart.

It was more than three weeks later that Nora's family arrived at the South Street Quay in New York. Her Da was still tall and handsome, though a walking skeleton (and yes, he had his fiddle with him), her Mam's beautiful crown of hair had turned white, and Nora was left with only one sister. Gentle Kate had succumbed to the fever and died while at sea.

It was a few days later that they found out the ticket agent's sister had died and there was no other family member to give the dresser to. It was Nora's forever!

Thou shalt not be afraid for the terror by night; nor for the arrow that flieth by day; nor for the pestilence that walketh in darkness; nor for the destruction that wasteth at noonday.

Psalms 91:5-6

GLOSSARY

An Gorda Mor. The Great Hunger.

A storin. Dear one.

Barm Brack. Nora's favorite bread, made with sugar, spices, and dried fruit. It was usually eaten for the festival of Imbolg (St. Brighid's Day) and other days.

Boxty cakes. A type of potato cake made by squeezing liquid from grated potatoes.

Brilla-bralla. Childish nonsense.

Cobh. A port city in County Cork, Ireland.

Creepie. Large stool.

Da. Father (familiar).

Delph. Type of earthenware known for its beauty and elegance.

Dia Dhuit. (Irish language) greeting; "Hello," "God be with you."

Fadge. Potato bread, usually eaten with butter.

Kinsale. City in West Cork, Ireland.

Loy. Large spade for digging potatoes.

Lumper. Potato variety, known for its golden color.

Mam. Mother (familiar).

Milesians. A Gaelic race that originated in Scythia, a region of southwestern Europe.

Mo Chraoibhin Cno. (Irish language) "My brown-eyed girl," "My Ireland."

Musha. (*Irish Language*) interjection; "indeed."

O maise, Dia linn. (*Irish language*) "God bless us."

Ocras. (*Irish language*) Hunger.

Praties. Potatoes.

Prod. Demeaning slang term for Irish Protestants.

Selkies. Humans who have taken on the form of seals (legendary).

Taise. Evil spirit.

Tuatha De Danann. Original inhabitants of Ireland (legendary).

Wherry. Light rowboat used for transporting passengers.